BUG OFF!

By Stewart C Lewis

TABLE OF CONTENTS

CHAPTER 1: A Knock on the Door

It all began when a guy knocked on my front door.

I was irritated. I don't like to be interrupted. I'd have been even more irritated if I'd have known that it would throw me into the middle of...but that's getting ahead of things. And how could I have anticipated anything that preposterous?

But I opened the door anyway, and leaned out.

It was a kid that looked like he was doing college and needed spare jobs to help pay for his meal tickets. He was skinny and badly dressed. He wore a Pirates baseball cap backward. I was glad about the hat. It meant he wasn't a guy from some Religious Sect.

"Hi there," he said. "My name is mumble-mumble." I confess, I wasn't paying attention. Frankly, I didn't care what his name was.

The kid went on, "I represent Jonathon Smith, Attorney. Are you Tom Palmer?"

"Why do you want to know," I asked.

"I have a letter for Tom Palmer from Attorney Smith." The kid displayed a big envelope he'd been holding under his arm.

It looked like a marketing package from an insurance company. "What's it about?" I asked.

"I dunno, I'm not authorized to read it, only to deliver it." He shrugged. "I don't think it's a subpoena or anything like that. You're Tom Palmer, aren't you?"

I confessed and held out my hand.

"Can I see some identification?" The kid asked.

"You gotta be kidding."

"No, Sorry, I'm required to see ID so I'm sure the right person gets the letter."

I gave up. I showed him my driver's license and took the letter. Here's what it said.

From: Jonathon Smith, Esquire
Smith, Martin and Gomez, Attorneys at Law, LLC
201 S Green Street, Suite 200
Locust, PA

To: Thomas R Palmer
12 Green Street
Locust, Pa
DOB: 05301978
DNA Acct 8NX4-Q92G-PPX1-0001

Dear Mr. Palmer,

If you are not Mr. Palmer as identified above, please return this letter immediately to the above referenced attorney.

If you are indeed the Mr. Palmer with the DOB, and etc., as noted above, well; you are not who you thought you were, and we have been looking for you for some time.

Now that you have been identified, it is imperative that you meet with us at the earliest possible time, in that we have information which is of the utmost importance to you.

Do not pass up this opportunity to change your life! Call for an appointment at once.

Yours truly,

Jonathon Smith, Esq.

I let this fester for a while, and then I checked the internet.   Sure enough, Smith, Martin, Gomez, specializing in Estates, Trusts, Missing Persons, Debt Forgiveness, etc.   Serving Locust, Pa and adjacent areas. Nice big web site. Four Stars on Angie's List.

And the letter cited my DNA Account number. That made me curious. How did they get my DNA Account number?

So I called. What else could I do? What would you do?

Even though I knew it was an Amway offer or something like that.

The lady on the phone said I could drop by the next morning.

Locust Daily Register, May 22: According to Locust Police Department spokesman, a Ms. Joan Cheffield was reported missing by her cousin, Jean Figuroa. Ms. Cheffield, who lived alone, was last seen Friday May 18 following dinner at the new McGregory's Burgers. Mrs. Figuroa stated "Joan should be easy to spot, since she's a large plus size. We know she must be in trouble because she's never before skipped a meal."

Chapter 2: Jonathon Smith, Esquire

I found Jonathon Smith, Esquire, of Smith, Martin and Gomez, Attorneys at Law, LLC, in an office on the 2nd Floor of the Green Street Office Complex, near the center of the town of Locust, Pa.

The building was mostly filled with a variety of medical purveyors. I noted I could get either a colonoscopy or a root canal there. Based on that, I didn't care for the aura of the building.

I told the dour little old lady at the front desk my name and she gave me a look like I'd stepped in something unpleasant. She consulted her computer monitor before leading me down a short hall to the second door on the left. She opened it, leaned in and whispered "Tom Palmer is here, Mr. Smith." She motioned me in.

He came around the desk like he was out to stab me with an outstretched hand. "Tom Palmer" he exulted, "Come in, come in!" He was short and stout but apparently used enthusiasm to compensate for lack of stature.

We fumbled through a handshake and got ourselves seated at opposite sides of the huge desk. I eyed him nervously; he sort of jiggled excitedly in his chair.

"Well," he began. "Tom Palmer!' He repeated. It seemed like he had to keep reminding himself who I was.

"We are so thrilled to have located you, Mr. Palmer! We have been searching for you ever since...well..." he paused, and sort of chuckled.

"Let me explain," he began over. "I am executor of the estate of Jack Forsome, who passed a month ago. He left quite a complex estate, let me tell you!"

I let him run on. I wasn't sure I could interrupt him anyway.

"It has been quite difficult, because much of the assets seem to be located in a very well secured vault beneath his residence, Greendale. We have been unable to enter the vault to inventory those assets as the vault was constructed to require a specific DNA code to permit entry. That DNA code is that of Jack Forsome himself." Jonathon Smith, Esquire paused to blow his nose.

"Can't you just get the code or a sample or something and open it with that?" I asked.

"Not quite. The mechanism requires an actual finger with the proper DNA, and while of course we thought to uh, well, borrow, a digit from the deceased, unfortunately the deceased was cremated, a bit prematurely, it seems. There is no digit to borrow."

"That's too bad," I said, "But I don't see how this concerns me."

"We have evidence that it most certainly does concern you, Mr. Palmer. You see, we believe your DNA can open the Forsome vault."

I was trying to think how that might be, when Jonathon Smith, Esquire said, "We believe you are Jack Forsome's son."

I blinked. "That would be news to me. I was raised by Clyde and Doris Palmer, who I always believed to be my parents. They never suggested otherwise."

He said, "I understand you haven't been given cause to think otherwise, but we do have evidence, and of course we've confirmed that your DNA is 99.99+% likely to be that of the direct descendant of Jack Forsome. In other words, Jack Forsome is definitely your father."

"Wait a minute. How do you know what my DNA is? That sample I sent in is supposed to be strictly confidential."

"Yes, it is. But your father – Dr. Forsome - happened to have certain resources that were able to assist him with finding a match of not more than two degrees of separation from his own DNA. So you see, we only learned of your existence very recently, after you submitted your DNA sample."

I thought 'Thank you Marie - maybe.' Marie is my cousin, and a huge ancestry buff. She is the one who talked me into sending in my DNA sample, about three months ago. I recall that we were both surprised at how different my DNA is from hers. She thought maybe the sample had gotten contaminated, or something, and wanted me to submit another sample. I hadn't done that yet. She was going to be floored to learn about my just discovered father.

"How did he die?" I asked. "Was it a long illness?"

"No. I understand he was quite healthy. He was found dead in his back yard, quite unexpectedly, one morning about four weeks ago."

"Was it a heart attack or something like that?"

"I don't believe the cause of death was conclusively determined. And the family refused an autopsy."

"Wait a minute. Your letter had my DNA number. How exactly did you get involved in all this?"

"I was hired by your father to contact you, among other legal services. He provided your DNA account information. Unfortunately we didn't succeed in locating you until after he had passed away."

"So he suddenly discovered that he had a son he'd never met, and then he died?"

"Yes, very unfortunate. I understand he was quite eager to meet you. When he learned about you, he immediately wrote a letter to your mother, a letter that was never sent, because he discovered she had already passed away."

"I guess I'll need to see that letter."

"Of course you do. It is in the possession of Sally Conners, Jack Forsome's sister. And I believe she is very eager to meet you, her newly discovered nephew. As are her children, your cousins that you've never met."

"Cousins. I have cousins? Do I have brothers or sisters?" I muttered, picturing these strangers greeting me, as surprised at the revelation as I was.

He shook his head, no. "No siblings, just cousins. And in any case, the crux of the matter is, uh, may I call you Tom?" Smith couldn't wait for my answer; "is confirming your parentage, and determining whether your finger will open the Forsome vault. We are eager to gather the parties involved with the estate and settle that very thing!"

He made a phone call and arranged for me to meet 'Aunt' Sally next. Then he handed me a business card that said:

IdentityDNA.Com
DNA tests available for all purposes:
Paternity, Ancestry, Health and More.
Results available in as little as one day.
All at a convenient location near You.

"I strongly suggest that you avail yourself of this service, promptly," he advised, "And be sure to have the results certified for use in court."

As I left he was proceeding to organize a meeting of the people involved with the estate, at Greendale, the Forsome residence, later that day.

On my way out the dour little old lady gave me a disapproving look. I had to check my shoes again.

Chapter 3: Aunt Sally

'Aunt' Sally Conners had a nice fourth floor condo in the Locust Square Over-55 Building, just down Green Street from Smith's office. She had grey hair and wore metal rimmed spectacles and a red sweater.

"My god you look just like my brother Jack!" she exclaimed as she let me in.

A huge TV was blaring on the far wall. I think it was a Soap Opera, because all the actors looked depressed. Aunt Sally pressed the mute button. "That's better," she said. "Now let's get down to the business at hand." She chuckled.

She walked to her desk, littered with papers and pill bottles. "When Smith called and said you were coming over, I got out this old photo of Jack." She fumbled absently through the papers on the desk. "Now I know it's here someplace...Oh, here it is!"

She handed me an old photo. "See how much you look like him!" She exclaimed. "I can see that you're his kid, and my long lost nephew! My goodness, it's exciting to meet you! Jack's boy!" She chuckled again. I guess I amused her.

"Uh, it's nice to meet you, too, Mrs. Conners." I said as I examined the photo. Jack Forsome sort of looked like me, I guess. Or rather I look like he used to, years ago. Although I never sported a moustache like his.

"Oh, please call me Aunt Sally," She insisted.

"Uh, nice to meet you, Aunt Sally,"

"That's better. I knew of your mother," Aunt Sally went on as we settled on her couch. "I was sure Jack was going to marry her. But then he got that big Government contract and became too busy. He took trips when he was out of touch for weeks on end. Your mother got tired of waiting for him and found another guy."

"That would be Clyde?"

"Yes. I suppose maybe she needed to get married because she was pregnant, although I didn't realize it at the time. And I didn't know about her having you until Jack told me about you, a couple of months ago." She chuckled. "I was quite surprised!"

"So you believe my mother got married because she had to," I said, cleverly.

"Yes, I looked it up on the Internet. The wedding was in March and you were born in August. You shouldn't fault her, you know, getting married was the responsible thing to do. Besides, it's possible she didn't know for sure which beau was your father. I believe she was seeing both Jack and Clyde for a time. I suppose she didn't tell you, did she?"

"No, this is all news to me."

"I think you should be quite pleased about this," Aunt Sally said. "You now have relatives you never knew about. And, as Jack's only direct descendent you might quite possibly inherit Jack's estate...He became quite wealthy, you know."

"I never heard of him until now so I don't know anything about him." I said. "He really didn't know about me?"

"I believe he only learned of you quite recently. He was an introvert and wasn't the kind to be much interested in people. Particularly once your mother married someone else. He was so involved with his work."

"What kind of work did he do?"

"I think he was an inventor of sorts. He developed some things the government wanted very badly. It was very secretive stuff. He built a big secret laboratory underneath his house where he spent most of his time. He rarely saw anyone except in the course of his work."

"What did he die from?"

"That's the funny thing, he was so healthy everybody thought he would outlive us all, and then bang, he dropped dead." She shook her head sadly. "And he was so looking forward to meeting you. You just never know, do you?"

"Life does have its funny turns," I agreed. "Attorney Smith said you have a letter that Dr. Forsome wrote to my mother."

"Oh yes, Jack's letter. I knew there was something else to tell you about, I just seem to keep forgetting things anymore. I have it here somewhere. It's sometimes hard to remember where you put things. I suspect I'm getting a bit absent-minded these days." She giggled pleasantly.

She had to rummage through a shoebox of papers and then two desk drawers before she came up with a blue envelope. "Here we are! I was to deliver it to your mother when we located her. But then she had passed before he did, so it was never delivered. I guess it's yours now."

I opened the envelope and took out the letter. It was handwritten:

Dearest Doris,

I write this to offer my sincerest apologies for treating you so badly. Things just got very complicated once the contract with Albertville was signed, and I was unable to get away from the responsibilities long enough to treat you as you deserve, and as my heart desired.

It is the greatest regret of my life that I lost you, but in retrospect it seems so inevitable. Although the times we had together were the most happy of times for me, I always thought you deserved someone who could give you more attention than I am capable of. I am consoled by the thought that you are better off with Clyde than with me.

So I understand why you married; and I wish the best of everything for all three of you. I would like to have learned that Tom is my son sooner, but I can't blame you for not telling me. I am hopeful of meeting him someday. I am now in a position where I could do a lot for him, but I understand why you'd rather I not confuse things. However, I promise you that I will provide for our son in the future.

Please forgive me.

Sincerely,

Jack Forsome

"Isn't that so very touching," Aunt Sally chimed in as I finished reading the letter. She chuckled and continued, "Your cousins Troy and Larry were quite upset when they learned about you. They are very concerned that they may not inherit all of Jack's things."

"My cousins?"

"Yes, my children. They've been gloating over Jack's estate like greedy pigs. I wouldn't be sorry for them to get left out because they don't deserve it...they're both selfish slackers who've never amounted to much." She laughed again. "Isn't it funny to hear a mother talk that way about her children? But they didn't get along with Jack. They take after their father, my late husband."

"So they're Jack Forsome's nephews. Won't their DNA open the vault?"

"No, their DNA is three degrees separated from Jack's. I am two degrees separate, as Jack's sibling. That's why neither my DNA nor my sons DNA will open the vault. Your DNA is only one degree separated from Jack." She chuckled. "Not that they didn't try to open the vault! They were so disappointed!"

'But shouldn't you be inheriting at least some of your brother's things?"

"Oh how nice of you to think so! But no, he left me out of his will because he set me up with a nice little trust fund years ago, so I'm quite well off. Besides, I'm too old to do anything useful with all that money. I spend most of my time with my nice beautiful 55 inch TV. And my DVR! It remembers all those things I seem to forget."

I glanced at the TV. The characters in the Soap that was playing on it still looked depressed, and now they seemed confused as well. Me too, I thought, wondering where all this was leading...

Chapter 4: My Cousins

A couple of middle-aged men bracketed the sidewalk, waiting for me as I left the Locust Square Over-55 Building. The taller thinner one wore a blue sports jacket and had a thin moustache, while the shorter heavier one sported a plaid vest and a Coors Light cap worn backwards. Both had a sharp pointed nose with a bend.

"So you must be Tom Palmer," the taller one said with an edge in his voice. "I'm Troy Conners, this is my brother Larry. You're claiming to be our cousin."

I wondered how they knew about me so quickly.

"Nice to meet you," I said, extending my hand. 'Let's all be friends,' I thought. Optimistically, as it turned out, since neither Troy nor Larry shook my hand. In fact, they ignored it.

"We have some information for you, Palmer," Troy said, pointing a finger at the center of my chest. "Explain it to him, Larry."

"You ain't gettin' one red cent from Uncle Jack's Estate!" Larry was clearly excited about this, as he blared the words at me. His spittle flew wildly. Luckily none landed on me.

Troy was nodding, confirming Larry's judgment. "That's the bottom line, Palmer." He went on before I decided how to respond. "Let me fill in some details: Your shyster Smith isn't executor of Jack Forsome's Estate, I am."

"Are you really?"

"Yes I am. And there's no law that requires us to check your DNA, so we're not gonna. In fact, we don't believe you're related at all. We believe Smith made it all up to horn in on Uncle Jack's Estate."

"Bu I never knew he might be my father. I didn't even learn about the estate until an hour or two ago," I protested. "And I'm not trying to horn in."

"Yeah, we're gonna buy *that* story," Troy went on. "And get this: even if you were related, your DNA wouldn't work the vault – your DNA is different from Uncle Jack's. The half you got from your mother doesn't match. Anyway, we have an expert coming to open the vault tomorrow, and you aren't invited."

"I thought there was to be a meeting there, later today."

"Nope, the meeting Smith tried to set up isn't gonna happen. We set him straight about that."

"What about the letter your mother showed me?"

"That letter is clearly a forgery. It would never hold up in court, not that it'll ever get that far. Sum it all up for him, Larry." Troy directed. Troy seemed to be in charge.

"Go back to whatever hole Smith dug you out of and keep out of our business or we'll hafta do somethin' serious about you, Palmer." Larry apparently spoke only in ultra-loud volume. This time he wiped the spittle off his chin with his sleeve.

Troy added, "And we plan to get a court order to keep you away from Uncle Jack's house. Get near the place and we'll have you arrested."

"Got the picture? Good. So long, Palmer," Larry concluded the conversation.

They headed away down the sidewalk, without waiting for my reply.

So the first time ever I meet my cousins, and we got along like a kitten and a pair of Jack Russell Terriers...it sucked. They even denied being my cousins, though their Mom seemed to think I was. And apparently Smith esquire had some explaining to do.

Chapter 5: Marty

I was considering confronting Smith about the inconsistencies in his story next, when my phone rang.

Hello

Hello my name is Marty Wilson and I have information you need to hear.

May I ask what number you are calling?

I'm calling Tom Palmer. That's you, isn't it?

How'd you get my number?

Never mind, just please listen to me. I was Dr. Forsome's Assistant and I knew him well. I know things you need to learn, and soon.

Well, go ahead.

Not over the phone. There are people who don't need to hear this stuff before things are more resolved. We will need to meet.

What the hell, I thought. He happened to be nearby, so I agreed to meet him at the bar in the Rose and Thorn Pub, which was around the corner on State Street.

Marty Wilson arrived at the entrance to the Rose and Thorn while I was parking my Honda. He was with a couple of kids, maybe ten years old, who continued down the street when he entered the bar. I followed him into the bar.

Marty Wilson is a thin and mousy sort of man, with dark narrow eyes darting here and there, never quite looking at me. We sat side by side at the bar. I had a Bloody Mary, why not? It seemed a Bloody Mary sort of day. He had a Martini.

"So what's your story?" I asked.

"I worked with your dad, Dr. Forsome, for a few years. I got to know him well, and there are things you need to know."

"What sorts of things? Did he know he had a son?"

"He didn't know about you until just a couple months or so ago, and he was flabbergasted to find out. He was really quite thrilled. He just wished that your mother had told him about you."

"So he didn't know my mother was pregnant? When they broke up?"

"They didn't break up. He got into responsibilities that took him away all the time, and finally she moved on. And, no; he never knew she was pregnant. When he found out, he wrote a letter to your mother, but then we discovered she had passed away."

"That would be the letter my Aunt Sally has?"

"Yes. He changed a bunch of things when he learned about you. He even wrote a new will. But then your parents had passed and we weren't able to locate you until just before he died." He sipped his Martini gingerly. I chugged the Bloody Mary.

"How did he die?" I was hoping for a clearer answer than I'd gotten so far.

"Officially, unspecified natural causes."

"Is there an unofficial version?"

"Kevin Dibbler thinks so."

"Who's Kevin Dibbler?"

"Delivery boy. He did a lot of work for your father. Groceries, and so on. He was at Greendale a lot."

"And what does he think?"

"I'll let him explain his theories." Wilson avoided the question. "Here's his address." He scribbled it on a napkin and handed it to me.

"But more importantly," He went on, "The things your father was involved with are the bigger problems. Much bigger problems. Your DNA is going to get you caught up in strange things. You're probably in serious danger." He looked around nervously.

"Strange things? Danger? From what? What kind of work did you do with him?"

"It was classified stuff. I'm not permitted to tell anyone."

"That's real helpful. You tell me I'm in danger, but you can't say from what."

"Yeah, sorry. Anyway, there's also some other important things that need to be resolved."

"Well clue me in, and I'll get right on it." The lack of real information from this guy was becoming irritating. "How did Dr. Forsome learn about me, anyway?"

"He had me monitoring the major genetic databases for matches with his DNA for years, and finally yours showed up. He realized immediately that Doris was your mother: 'It can only be Doris', he said. But then we couldn't find you or your parents, you must have moved and not left forwarding addresses. After Dr. Forsome passed away, his attorney Smith and I kept looking. I tried to involve your Cousins, but they laughed, told me to forget it, and more or less just threw me out." He snorted. "They were very unfriendly."

"They weren't very nice to me, either." I agreed.

"By the way, Dr. Forsome left these things for me to give you." He slid a paper bag across the bar at me. I looked inside: there was a pair of sunglasses, thick and dark, and a water pistol.

"He left me a toy squirt gun? Are you kidding?" I took it out and looked closer. It was red and yellow translucent plastic. The body was shaped like Flash Gordon's rocket ship, with a small fin on the back. Three blue rings circled the body. The handle had a neon green hand-shaped grip, with a trigger you squeeze to shoot the water. There was a rubber plug on the back end where you refilled the thing. I stuffed it in my jacket pocket.

I took a quick glance at the sunglasses before shoving them in my inside jacket pocket. They were wraparound sport sunglasses with a dark blue mirror finish on the lenses, and a thick black heavy duty frame.

"They're for the aliens," Marty Wilson said nervously. "Don't you believe in UFOs?"

I snorted. "Nobody believes in aliens. They're always a hoax."

Just then a tall guy in a severe dark suit entered the bar, pocketing his sunglasses as he came in. He looked around and spotted us, then sat at a stool at the far end of the bar. Marty Wilson abruptly said, "I gotta go. Talk to you later." He slid quickly off the stool and hurried out the door. I finished my Bloody Mary, watching the tall guy in the dark suit. He casually looked around and then without ordering anything, he left too.

After lunch, I decided to look up Kevin Dibbler since his address was just a few blocks away. I confess to feeling curious about the cause of death. After all, if this guy was really my father, I shared his genetics.

Kevin Dibbler turned out to have the third floor walk-up apartment over Bonita's Modern Wave Hair & Nail Salon. You had to enter from the back of the building. I climbed the stairs and knocked, puffing from the exercise.

It took a minute, but then the door opened and it was the kid who had delivered the envelope to me yesterday afternoon. He still wore the Pirates cap, backwards.

"Kevin Dibbler," I said.

"Oh hey, man, yeah. You're the dude I dropped Attorney Smith's package with yesterday, right? How'd that turn out?" He was holding a small pipe, which he pointed at me in recognition.

"It delivered quite a surprise," I admitted. "It turns out that my father isn't my father, because Dr. Jack Forsome is my father."

"Oh Wow! Dr. Jack is your father? I knew he was looking for his kid. And it's you, huh? Now that you mention it, you do kinda look like him."

"So I've been told. I gather you knew him pretty well...mind if I ask a couple questions?"

"No problem. Wanna step in?"

"Thanks. How did he die?" I asked as I entered the apartment.

He suddenly looked defensive. "You're not going to believe me. The others don't."

"Just tell me."

"An alien murdered him."

I bit my tongue. Well I didn't really bite it, but then I didn't shout out, 'Whoa man, you must be playing with a few cards missing from your deck,' like I was thinking. Instead I said, "You mean like a 'little green man' alien? What makes you think that?"

"Actually it was a blue scaly alien. I delivered groceries the night before your father passed, and it was there. I think it was waiting for him."

So by now I'm suspecting that Kevin was maybe a little off from the reality most of us live in. "Really? Do you see a lot of aliens?" I prompted.

"Some. I sense them rather than see them, though. And they smell."

"I guess that sounds, uh, logical." I had to bite my tongue again.

"Yeah. It was Peaches and Willow that clued me in to the aliens, at first," Kevin explained. "Dr. Jack's cats. I feed them, and they talk to me, you know, animal talk. They warned me about the aliens. You know, cats know stuff like that, right?"

""Yeah, cats are strange creatures." I had no disagreement about that. "Are there a lot of aliens around Greendale?" I asked as I looked around the apartment. It was one big room plus a bath and a bedroom. There was a lot of debris scattered about.

"Yeah, the place must be an alien magnet. It was the cats who taught me to sense them, so after a while I could tell when they were there, even though I couldn't see them. I can smell them. Dr. Jack agreed, you know, when I told him about all the aliens hanging around."

The walls of Kevin's apartment were covered with posters, pictures, and paintings. All featuring aliens. Big and small aliens, green and blue, humanoid, lizard and insect aliens. "You have quite a collection of aliens here," I commented, indicating the walls. "Have you seen all of these?"

"No, just a couple. Mostly I can smell them. The ones I've seen, I don't think they're good aliens."

"Especially if they killed Dr. Forsome," I added.

"Exactly." Kevin nodded and went on. "What I'm really hoping for someday is to meet up with a good alien that's a hot space chick. That would be really cool."

"Sure would," I had to agree. Some of the aliens on the walls were clothed. Some were naked. Some were *very* naked, if you get my meaning. I saw where Kevin got his thoughts about a hot space chick.

"Oh hey, I'm not being polite. You wanna little hit on this?" Kevin waved his pipe at me.

At that, I figured I had enough information from Kevin. "Thanks, but no." I told him. "I have to drive this afternoon.   Actually I'm late, so I gotta go. Thanks for the info." I let myself out.

Chapter 6: Meeting Sophia

I eased down the three flights of Kevin's steps and started toward my car, still parked downtown, when a red Toyota sedan pulled over beside me. Down came the passenger side window, revealing a blonde driver leaning my way.

"Tom Palmer," she said, "Get in the car".

"What?" I wasn't sure I heard right.

"I said, get in the car. Please." She leaned over and pushed the door open. I noticed she filled the sweater nicely.

I should have been suspicious, but not every day do I get picked up by a sexy blonde. In fact, this was the first time ever. So I got in the car.

"How do you know who I am?" I asked.

"You're in the paper." She showed me the Greater Locust Area Shopping News as she accelerated away from the curb.   "You've become quite a celebrity here in Locust."

The Greater Locust Area Shopping News had a picture of me on the front page, over a headline: '*New Heir Muddies Forsome Estate Settlement*.' The story went on, complete with quotes from Jonathon

Smith, Esquire, spokesman for Tom Palmer. According to my spokesman, I was eager to develop a positive relationship with the Locust Community.

Things seemed to be rapidly snowballing on me. I didn't see how I was going to get back to my crossword puzzles, the way things were piling up.

"So then, we know who I am, now who are you?" I asked the blonde.

"Sophia Johnson." She held out a hand for me to shake. "Glad to meet you."

"It's nice to meet you, too, Sophy."

"No," she corrected. "It's Sophee-ah, not Sophee."

"Sorry, Sophee-ah. Do you often pick up strange celebrities?" I asked.

She blushed. "Well, I saw you standing there and you looked like a nice person, and so I just did it. I'm sorry; I hope you don't mind too much." She turned the corner onto Acorn Street and accelerated smoothly.

"So long as it's not a kidnapping. I doubt if anyone would put up ransom for me."

"Oh no, it's robbery." She dropped her voice. "Give me all your money and I'll let you live." She laughed.

I laughed too. "Uh, not to be pushy but where are we going? And why?"

"Okay Tom," she said, "I'm going to be straight with you. I'm looking for your business. I'm a real estate agent and I want you to list Greendale, the Forsome residence, with me. I shouldn't do this but I'm willing to negotiate the commission in order to get the business. I'd like to look the property over with you. We can generate some ideas on how to move it most profitably."

"Well, I'm sorry, Sophia, but as things stand right now I'm not sure of inheriting anything, and I'm not even allowed on the property. So we can't just drive up and walk in as if I owned the place outright. As a matter of fact, I've never even seen the place."

"I thought it might be a bit complicated" she said. "But I think you should at least take this opportunity to look at the property. Sometimes you just have to seize the day."

"So far the day has been sort of seizing me. Do you believe in aliens? I was warned about aliens today, among other things."

"Aliens? You mean like UFOs and such?"

"Yeah, I think so."

"Nobody believes in that nonsense but wierdos and such. You don't believe in little green men, do you?" She looked at me with concern.

"I've never had reason to before. But then, I never had reason to suspect that my father had a big estate that I've never seen, either. Now, who knows what's what."

"As far as aliens visiting Earth, the universe is far too big for that to happen, so you can forget about aliens being a problem." she said. "And about the rest, I understand why you might be feeling just a bit overwhelmed. Maybe taking a look at the house will help you get your feet back on the ground. It's a beautiful property." Sophia drove fast, but neatly.

"Do you know where it is?"

"Of course...it's just down the street." She pointed to a tall stone fence running along the left side of the road. "That's the fence that goes all the way around it. About ten acres, size of the grounds. Lots of woods, as you can see."

She turned left and followed along the fence. It was interrupted by an imposingly large closed iron gate. Behind the gate a driveway wound through a grove of trees that blocked a view of the house.

"I guess that settles that...I don't have a key or code for the gate." I said. "We can't get in."

"Sure, there's a locked gate," Sophia said, "but I know where there's a hole in the fence. Since the house is vacant, we should have no problem taking a quick look around.'

She took a quick glance at me to see how I reacted to this. "There may be a dog but I have my tranquilizer gun." She giggled.

"Oh, then in that case we should be safe," I said. I thought she was kidding about the tranquilizer gun. And, I don't know why on earth I should have thought breaking into the house was a reasonable thing to do, but I agreed to do it with her. The day was already bizarre, so why not do something crazy.

Sophia u-turned neatly and parked the car beside a collection of bushes between the road and the fence. The break in the fence was behind the bushes. We squeezed through.

So picture me following this blonde in tight dark slacks through the woods behind the Forsome house. At least she wore sensible shoes...I think they were sneakers. Figures.

There was a large backyard, the size of about half a football field. The end near the house had a big barbeque fireplace. The driveway came along the other side of the yard until it curved toward the front of the house. We followed along a row of bushes that edged the other side of the backyard, until we reached the back of the house. I took off my jacket because things had warmed up in the late afternoon sun.

A small porch led to a locked back door, and beside it narrow steps led down to a cellar door. It was unlocked, so naturally, in we went.

Chapter 7: The Vault

The cellar was a large empty room with the usual appliances – furnace, water heater – and stairs leading up. We went up the stairs and managed to tour through most of the house. It was big, with 4 brms, 3 bths, drm, nice ktch. All very nice, large rooms, all very typical and normal looking though a bit sparse of furnishings. Like a bachelor's place.

The most unusual room was the oversized den. It had a large desk and credenza, and bookcases heavily laden all around. A variety of complex electronics covered the work surfaces. But the main curiosity was a huge metal door which looked just like a bank vault. It took up half of the wall opposite the only door into the room. I laid my jacket on the desk while we looked around.

Sophia and I were at the vault door, inspecting it, when my cousins burst into the room. They were followed by a large official looking man. He looked like a cop, carrying all that cop-like equipment loaded on his belt.

"Caught you now, Palmer," Larry spat out.

Troy had more details. This seemed the norm with my cousins. "We knew you'd come here. So it didn't take a genius to set up a trap and catch you red handed. We left the cellar door unlocked and you fell for it, stupid. Now you're caught trespassing, and we're gonna press charges. You and your bimbo here are going to jail. By the time you get out, I'll have Uncle Jack's estate all settled!"

"Now just a minute," protested Sophia, "You can't do that! We're here on business, I'm a registered real estate agent and Mr. Palmer is considering listing this property for sale. We're merely reviewing the property in preparation for advertising. That's not trespassing." She waved a commanding finger at Troy. He seemed momentarily mesmerized by her finger.

While she talked, I was still looking at the vault door. There was a curious mechanism featuring a metal plate on the wall beside the vault door. And centered on the plate was a hole that looked just big enough for a finger. The little light above it was glowing red.

"He won't be listing it for sale because it ain't his to sell," blurted Larry.

Troy said, "Let me introduce you to Special Deputy Fred Underhill, who will be arresting both of you for illegal trespass." He pointed to the big guy.

Deputy Underhill stepped toward me, removing the handcuffs from his belt. He was a lot bigger than me. I wasn't about to wrestle with him.

I seemed to be out of good choices. So I did what popped into my head... I stuffed my index finger deep into the hole in the wall, before my cousins or Deputy Underhill could interrupt. At least I'd find out something before I got arrested, I thought, optimistically.

The red light above my finger in the hole turned green with a quiet beep. The vault door responded with a loud click that reverberated through the room. Everybody froze at the noise, stopping all action while waiting to see what the click meant. It was followed by a loud, grinding, whirring noise, like heavy wheels turning. We all stared.

Then the huge vault door swung inward, slowly and majestically.

"Well, open sesame!" I exclaimed, for the moment thoroughly pleased with myself.

We could all see into the room beyond the door. It was large and empty. Empty, that is, except for the helicopter, sitting in the center of the room. Well, it was not really a helicopter, but something that looked like a yellow and blue coin operated thing you'd find outside a Kmart. You put your four year old in it, insert a quarter and the kid gets happily shaken for two minutes.

"Look! There's nothing in there!" Larry shouted. I was still staring at the helicopter but I could sense the flying spit behind me.

"So much for all the valuable stuff you thought you might score here, Palmer." Troy said. He seemed delighted. "This is hilarious. There's nothing in the famous vault, but a stupid toy. You should get in it, Palmer, so we can take your picture looking stupid, before you go to jail for trespassing. The Shopping News will really love you then!"

While Larry and Troy were laughing at their cleverness, I thought 'What the hell, what do I have to lose?' and so I got in the helicopter. I slung myself through the open side of the 'copter and onto the plastic seat. It was just large enough that I wasn't squeezed like a sardine.

"That's great, hold that pose!" Troy enthused, getting his iPhone ready to shoot me. Larry was still laughing. All four of them - Troy, Larry, Sophia and Deputy Underhill - crowded the vault doorway, watching me settle onto the plastic seat.

There was a pair of joysticks to the left and right, and a green button at the center of the dashboard. I pressed the green button.

The thing began to hum loudly, abruptly cutting off my cousin's mirth. Suddenly, thick transparent windows appeared from somewhere behind me and rapidly slid shut, completely enclosing me. Meanwhile, the seat altered itself somehow, softening and conforming itself comfortably to my body. I settled in.

Looking out, I noticed that everybody had their mouth hanging agape with surprise. They all seemed to be shouting, as I could see their wildly flapping mouths, although I couldn't hear them. Soundproofing? Looks of disbelief spread across their faces. I could read Larry's lips, however: "Where the f*** did he go!"

Then inside the helicopter a smooth female voice said to me, quietly, calmly, "The Invisibility Module has been engaged."

Could it be that they couldn't see me or the helicopter? Had I disappeared? I thought it must be some kind of optical trick. Things don't just disappear.

The soothing female voice went on, "Now securing the vault," she announced. The huge vault door wheeled shut, separating me from the other four people.

Chapter 8: Pinco F-1

I had thought the day up to now had been really weird, but consider my present situation. I sat enclosed in a bright yellow and blue arcade ride helicopter, seemingly invisible, locked in a huge vault, and wondering what to do next. Panic seemed a good choice, but before I could act on it the voice inside the helicopter said to me, "I sense that you are a new operator and are somewhat confused."

"Yeah, you got that right," I replied.

"I am Emma BCI-12," the voice went on. "I am the built-in control intermediary for the TeeDee that you currently occupy. Dr. Forsome recently amended the activation system, creating the possibility that someone other than he might meet the requirements for activating and operating the TeeDee. You have met his criteria."

"TeeDee?" I asked.

"Transportation Device," Emma said. "You may tell me your transportation requests and I will carry them out as best I can."

"Oh. Of course. Where did Dr. Forsome usually go in the, uh...TeeDee?" I asked.

"He went most often to Pinco F-1," Emma said. "Shall I take you there?"

"Peeko F1. What the hell is that? Is it a long trip?"

"Pinco F-1," she said deliberately, so I'd get it right next time. "Pinco F-1 is the Primary Interstellar Communication Facility on this planet. We should arrive in less than 15 minutes."

"The name Pinco has unfortunate political connotations, you know," I said.

"I do not understand the phrase, unfortunate political connotations. Is the word 'Pinco' offensive to you?"

"Not me, but to some," I said wisely. I decided to play along. "OK, let's go there." I wasn't convinced that we were actually going to go anywhere.

The TeeDee seemed to begin moving slightly, turning to head away from the vault door. Then it accelerated directly through the back wall of the vault, and into the open air outside the house. 'How did it go through a wall', I wondered. Once outside, it accelerated enormously, rocketing upward into the sky.

Quickly we leveled out, surprisingly far above ground. Despite how fast we seemed to be going there was no sensation of either motion or noise. I was still thinking maybe we really hadn't moved from the vault, but if so, the video effects were amazing. I could have Google and Apple fighting over the rights to this software.

I was just beginning to enjoy the experience, when Emma said, "Sensors indicate that an enemy patrol has spotted our ascent. You will need to prepare for confrontation."

Emma informed me that while she was not programmed for 'confrontations', the car was equipped with weapons that would need to be aimed and fired by me. The two joysticks on the left and right armrests had big red buttons on top, where your thumbs rest. I hung onto one with each hand. Crosshairs appeared on the windows in front of me. They moved as I manipulated the joysticks. This is great, I thought, just like an arcade game.

"The enemy approaches us from behind," Emma said calmly. "I will rotate the TeeDee so that you face backwards, giving you a clear line of fire on the hostile craft."

The car spun dizzily and then I was looking backward. No fooling, there was a flying saucer pursuing us. It looked like two silver pie plates welded together. It had a protruding lump on the top, with shiny black windows making it look like a cockpit. Colored lights spun dizzily around the outer rim of the thing. It bobbed and weaved as it raced closer to us.

Disbelief made me hesitate. It couldn't really be a flying saucer. It came closer, and then a white glowing blob like a messy snowball burst from a node on the front of the saucer. It careened directly at us. The saucer bounced away from us, pushed by the recoil.

I gasped, expecting impact of some kind when the white blob hit, but it just burst open around the car, surrounding us with a brilliant rainbow flash of light. Quickly the light dissipated into thin air. Apparently we had somehow been shielded from any damage. Great video effects again, I thought.

"You must destroy the enemy quickly because I am unable to divert more than two or three additional hits like that," Emma warned dryly. "In which case we will be incinerated. I recommend that you try to hit the saucer before it gets back into firing range."

I wasn't looking forward to being incinerated, so I squeezed the joysticks tighter and focused, thanking goodness for all my video game experience. I manipulated the sticks until the crosshairs lined up on the saucer. Then I thumbed the red buttons.

A sparkling red tinted donut seething with energy spurted from the front of the car, and rocketed toward the saucer. At the last moment the saucer tried dodging, but the donut swerved and successfully hit. The saucer flashed and sparkled in a bright rapidly expanding reddish haze, then coalesced into what looked like a big clump of water droplets. Immediately it began to fall, looking like a little rain shower, and then it was gone. No sign of the saucer remained.

"Wow," I exclaimed, "That was really cool, almost like it was real!"

"It was real," Emma corrected me. "We were attacked by a flying saucer. Congratulations on your efficient shooting."

"Oh, come on, this thing is just a really good arcade ride of some sort, because there aren't any UFOs, really. Do you suppose I should remain in here until my cousins' leave? By the way, how do I get back to the vault?"

"Perhaps you should ask Patricia," Emma said. The TeeDee rotated, turning me to look forward again. I nearly jumped out of my seat because directly and unavoidably ahead of us was the straight up and down rocky side of a mountain, and we were about to crash into it.

I braced for the impact. Incredibly the TeeDee passed right through the mountainside like it wasn't there. For a second all was black around us, and then we careened into a large, well-lit hanger. We decelerated rapidly, and eased softly onto a pedestal obviously meant to cradle the TeeDee. The windows seemed to evaporate noiselessly, leaving the car sides open.

"Welcome to Pinco F-1," Emma announced. "Patricia normally stores herself in the recharge room. I hope you enjoyed your trip, and please ride with me again soon."

I dismounted. The car went quiet, although the hum it made when running had been barely noticeable.

But where the hell was I? I certainly wasn't in the vault anymore. Or was I? Probably this was just another room in the vault. I wasn't sure. I decided to explore.

Chapter 9: Patricia

I looked around the hanger. Besides Emma and the TeeDee, three other helicopter-like vehicles sat on their respective pedestals, all looking in serious disrepair compared with Emma's TeeDee. The place had a high domed ceiling, and three featureless walls including the mountainside that we had come through. It seems awfully large to be part of the vault, I thought. I rapped a knuckle on the wall we had come through and it felt like a hard acrylic of some kind. The other walls looked like the same stuff.

The fourth wall had three doors. Which door has the tiger behind it, I wondered. No, bad attitude; it was sure to be some nice prize. I decided on the door on the right, first. It was a storage room, with shelves piled up with pieces of this and that. I suspected they might be parts for the vehicles in the hanger, but my accounting and finance background left me helpless to identify any of it.

The door on the left led to an office. It had a big desk, file cabinets, a bookcase, and a sofa bed. A coffee machine sat unused on a side table, along with varied supplies. There was a little collection of mugs, all clean except for a thin layer of dust. Looked like nobody had used them in quite a while.

The desk was mostly uncluttered but my eye caught sight of a handwritten note. I picked it up but before I could read it, I heard a noise in the hanger. I put the note in my pocket and went to investigate, but I found nothing.

The center door led to a short hallway with two doors across from each other, at the end of the hall away from the hanger. The door to the left was filled with complex equipment reminiscent of a mainframe computer, or perhaps the bridge of a submarine. It had lots of control panel kinds of displays, and I couldn't tell what any of it was for.

The final room was reminiscent of an examination room at a doctor's office. A woman was lying face up on a table in the middle of the room, covered with a white sheet. Patricia, apparently. The table she lay on looked like an operating room table, with tubes and wires going here and there. A machine on the wall had a display that was going "Beep....beep....beep"

Patricia looked to be motionless, like she was deep in a coma. The sheet covered everything, except her face and feet. A large cable seemed to be attached to her stomach through an opening in the sheet. Her dark colored hair was to my right, her feet to the left.

I stepped into the room for a closer look, trying to see if she was breathing. I let the door swing shut behind me. When it closed a bell rang softly. "Ding-dong. Ding-dong," it said. 'Uh oh,' I thought, 'what did I set off now?'

At the sound of the bell Patricia sat straight upright and turned to me. "Hello, Dr...." she started, then hesitated when she realized I was not who she apparently expected. Suddenly indignant, she demanded "Who the hell are you? Where's Dr. Forsome? How did you get here?" The sheet fell to her waist and...well, she seemed to be naked. And yes, the cable was connected to a socket in her belly button.

It took me a minute to answer the easy question first. "Emma brought me." That got her to relax a bit, so I added, "I'm afraid Dr. Forsome has passed away."

"Oh my goodness, I'm so sorry," she exclaimed. "But now I can see it...you're his son. You look like him. He had prepared for this eventuality" She turned and slid off the table, wrapping the sheet carefully around her shoulders like a bathrobe. She reached under it and detached the cable which had been plugged into her belly button. She was petite, perhaps 5' 1" or so, and quite slender. Long black hair cascaded around her shoulders. Her eyes were a bright green.

She fastened her belly-button cable into a docking bracket under the table, and stepped forward, reaching toward me with her index finger. Surprised, I pulled back. "Do not be afraid." She said, and I let her touch my arm. She pressed it firmly, for just a moment.

"I'm…not quite sure who I am, right now." I stumbled. "But my name is Tom Palmer."

"I know who you are. Your DNA" She held her finger up, showing a small red spot on the tip, "confirms that you are the direct offspring of Dr. Jack Forsome. As such, you will be assuming Dr. Forsome's responsibilities." She was all business now. "I will need to communicate with Skudas Dorval first, to clarify the situation and receive advice on how to proceed. Please follow me, Tom Palmer."

Patricia briskly led us across the hall into the room with all the machinery.

"What responsibilities?" I asked, trailing after her. "Who's Skippy Duval?" I was suffering from serious information overload. "What situation?" The questions kept coming. And so far, the answers didn't make sense.

"Skudas Dorval," she corrected. "He's the GPB Agent – the Galactic Policy Board, that is - for this sector."

"Of course, why didn't I know that?"

"You didn't know because his role with this planet is totally confidential...." She paused, glancing at me while she fiddled with something on a control panel. "Oh, I see, you are being cynical. I'm sorry but I am not designed to be amused by cynicism, Tom Palmer." She twisted a dial on the control panel, then picked up a cable and stuck the loose end of it deep into her left ear.

"What on earth are you doing with that cable?" I asked, shocked at her action.

"I am about to receive a transmission from Skudas Dorval, which will update our situation and suggest a course of action compatible with the policies of the GPB." She flipped a final switch on the control panel and rapid series of bells, whistles, beeps and so on rattled about the room. "Oops," she said, "Not quite plugged all the way in." She jiggled the cable end in her ear and the noise stopped, but Patricia went into a trance, a vacant stare on her face.

After an uncomfortably long period of silence while she stood catatonically, I asked "Are you OK? What's happening?" More dumb questions. No response. I was getting nervous. I had way too many unanswered questions. Patricia seemed to be the only source of answers, and here she stood like a statue.

I finally decided to see if I could shake her out of it, but just as I reached for her she blinked and her green eyes focused in on me. She sighed and removed the cable from her ear.

"I'm afraid it's bad news," She said.

"Funny how that's not a surprise," I quipped.

"I'm not sure how that would be funny...oh, more cynicism," She said. "You know, while cynicism relieves a certain narcissistic need, it rarely contributes to solving the tasks at hand," She lectured me.

"Gotcha. I'll try to control it from now on."

She continued despite my interruption, "The tasks have become considerably more compelling for your planet since I last met with Dr. Forsome, about a month ago. According to reports intercepted by

Skudas Dorval, the Krylki mothership has arrived on Earth."

Frankly I didn't know what to say. I suspected Patricia was delusional. Or was this just part of an arcade ride? I was getting tired of the 'aliens' nonsense. "And I suppose you're from outer space?" I asked her.

"I was assembled locally, if that's what you mean"

"Made in the USA?"

"The software which operates my physical form was provided by the GPB – the Galactic Policy Board. In that respect, I am as you say 'from outer space."

"I'll have to introduce you to Kevin Dibbler...he's looking for a hot space chick."

"I am not familiar with that expression, hot space chick. Are you referring to cooked poultry?"

I shook my head no. She went on, "I am dependent on you, the galactic representative, since my purpose is to serve as your advisor regarding GPB business."

I was annoyed that none of this seemed to make any sense, so finally I said, "Listen, I think it just might be best if I leave you to your equipment and so on so you can deal with the kracker problem however you want. How do I get out of here, and get back to Locust, Pennsylvania?"

"Krylki," she corrected. "Emma can of course transport you anywhere you want, anytime, but that would not be advisable right now, Tom Palmer."

I headed for the door. "It seems very advisable to me, so see you later. "

Patricia followed me into the hanger. "You must realize that you don't yet understand the seriousness of the situation," she protested. "And your presence here confirms your genetic responsibility."

I noted the look of dismay on her face as I clambered into the TeeDee and pressed the green button. Was I making a mistake? There are no aliens, right? I decided that's how I was going to play this game.

The windows closed in around me and I instructed Emma "Dr. Forsome's house, please."

In moments we had whisked through the side of the mountain, cruised back to the house and settled gently onto the docking pedestal in Dr. Forsome's vault.

Your Local Locust Metro Newscast, 6 PM May 23: Several witnesses in the western suburbs report seeing a peculiar flash of light in the sky. Some of the witnesses claim they saw what appeared to be a flying saucer just before the explosion. Stay tuned for further details as this story develops.

Chapter 10: Out of the Vault

I was out of the helicopter before the humming had completely stopped. My first concern was getting out of the vault since I was closed inside. My second concern was the gang waiting to arrest me for trespassing. Third, what had happened to Sophia while I was gone? Meanwhile I was trying to put the UFO nonsense out of my mind.

I was relieved to discover an inside release for the vault door, and it wheeled itself open without difficulty. I was even more relieved to see Sophia standing in the den, staring at me with a huge perplexed look on her face. And even better, I didn't see any of the others. I stepped out of the vault into the den. The vault door must have a proximity sensor or something because it closed behind me, with a solid 'thunk.'

"Where did you go? What happened to you? Are you alright? "   Sophia had trouble stopping her torrent of questions. "That was astonishing, you seemed to disappear then the vault door slammed shut. Your cousins are beside themselves."

"I think it's just a very effective arcade ride." I threw out. "I took a ride and shot up some aliens then the ride ended. We could probably sell the thing to Disney or Universal or somebody."

"You sure had us all on edge," she said. "Your cousins are outside looking for you while the Deputy keeps watch on the den door so I don't escape. But they don't seem concerned much about me, it's you they're after. They didn't even ask my name."

We tried the den door. Strangely it was not locked, and the Deputy was nowhere in sight. We snuck our way to the cellar door, where we had got in. We were out on the steps with a clear path to Sophia's car when the bright daylight made me remember the sunglasses and squirt gun given to me by Marty Wilson. I had put my jacket on the desk in the den, and had left them in it.

I sent Sophia ahead to start the car and went back for the glasses and squirt gun. On the way back through the cellar I encountered two cats, meowing insistently. Irritated, I told them to go tell Kevin their problems, as I hurried out the door.

I was just sliding the glasses on my face as I mounted the cellar steps, when I heard Larry yelling, "There he is! Stop right there, Palmer!"

Larry and Troy were rounding the corner of the house to my right. "Get him, deputy," Troy shouted. I looked to my left and here came the deputy around the other corner.

Then the glasses slid neatly into place, filtering my sight. Seen through the blue lenses, Deputy Underhill looked suddenly hazy, then transformed into a tall blue creature with huge bulging eyes and noseless face. It had big red lips around a gaping mouth. I was reminded of the creature from the black lagoon, except it was blue, not black.

The thing drew an odd looking weapon from its side and aimed at me. A bolt of white flashing light flew at me but burst around me without harmful impact, and rapidly dissipated into thin air. The creature holstered its' weapon and came running at me, making a loud sound like an angry dog's growl. I saw clearly that it had lots of long sharp teeth gnashing at me.

Without thinking I drew the squirt gun and shot it at the creature. A flashing sparkling blue donut a yard across burst from the water gun and almost instantly enveloped the blue creature. He seemed to pose there for a couple seconds, like an actor glowing in the spotlight. Then there was some sizzling and flashing and abruptly the creature simply dissolved into what looked like water, falling Ker splash into a large puddle on the ground.

I was giving the squirt gun a second astonished look when Troy and Larry arrived beside me.

"Did you see that!" yelled Larry. "It turned into a monster!" He was literally jumping up and down.

"It couldn't be. It was Deputy Underhill, right? What have you done, Palmer, you killed him!" Troy exclaimed.

"Killed who?" I asked, pointing to the puddle of water. I was still registering what happened. Deputy Underhill had turned into an alien when I put on the glasses. The squirt gun had shot it just like Emma's guns had shot the saucer. No trace left, nothing to raise questions. "There's no dead body," I pointed out.

"Where did it go?" Larry cried. He ran over and splashed in the puddle of water.

Meanwhile, Troy was busy with his iPhone. In a moment he held it up and announced, "The Locust Police Department is sending a car. They say there's no Deputy Underhill working for them, or that they've ever heard of. Who was that guy, Palmer, and what did you do to him?"

I tried calling it like I saw it. "Here's how it looked to me. He was a big blue alien disguised like a cop and I shot him dead with my ray gun, before he could kill me. And I did it without leaving a single shred of evidence." It didn't sound very believable even as it came out of my very own mouth.

"Don't be a wise guy, Palmer," said Larry. "We're not stupid. There ain't no such thing as aliens." But I could hear the doubt in his voice.

"Yeah, what we saw musta been a trick of the sunlight, reflecting off the windows or something like that," added Troy. "The deputy will turn up soon and then we'll get some answers."

I confronted them. "You saw it, didn't you. You saw him turn into a big blue alien when I shot him."

"It musta been an optical illusion, that's all." Troy insisted. "And the Locust police will get here in a minute. Then, we'll clear this up." He didn't sound very certain.

"Well, I won't be here when the police arrive," I announced. I took off in the direction of Sophia's Toyota. I dashed through the trees and climbed through the hole in the fence. I burst out of the bushes hiding the break in the fence, right beside the Toyota.

Sophia was standing beside the car with the door open. She was clearly surprised by my sudden appearance. In a knee jerk reaction, she raised the little pistol she was carrying and it went off. I felt a jab of pain in my hip.

"Oh shit!" I heard Sophia exclaim, a look of dismay spreading across her face. I didn't answer because I was quickly falling asleep.

Chapter 11: Waking up

I was having a bad dream. Women kept staring at me with dismay. Guys were yelling at me. A big blue monster with huge teeth kept reappearing no matter how many times I killed it. And something kept saying grzzz, grzzz, grzzz, on and on. I wanted it all to go away; I just wanted my crossword puzzle and my morning bowl of rice krispies. My usual routine.

With that thought, I awoke with a start, staring at the ceiling. But whose ceiling? Not mine; I was not in my own bed. I turned to the left, where there was a source of light. A window with pink frilly lacey curtains, daylight shining in from outside. Definitely not my window.

I twisted to the right and there was a big scramble of blonde hair almost in my face. Then I recognized the grzzzing sound...she was snoring. I was at a loss for explanations for a moment. Waking up in a strange bed with a blonde is rather spectacularly out of my normal range of experience. In a panic I quick checked to see if I was clothed...I was. I wondered momentarily if I should be happy about that, or not. And was she clothed?

Then things started coming back to me, in reverse order. Sophia tranquilizing me was the last thing I could remember from yesterday. Before that had been the big blue thing and the astonishment on Larry and Troy's faces. Patricia and Emma. My father's estate.

Reflexively I pinched myself. It hurt, so evidently it had all been real. Trying to sort it all out, I was having trouble deciding what to do next.

Sophia solved the problem for me. She snorted conclusively and rolled onto her back, bumping into me in the process. Her eyes snapped open, taking in me and the daylight streaming in the window.

"Uh, good morning, I think," I greeted her.

"Omigod! I'm so sorry," she exclaimed, sitting upright. "It was an accident, I swear! I heard a dog and the bushes moved and the gun just went off and...Are you okay?" I think she had on the same sweater and jeans from yesterday.

"Well, so far I seem to be okay. Where are we?"

"When you collapsed, I brought you here. This is my apartment. I didn't know what else to do, so it was a good thing Mr. Wilson came by and he was so helpful getting you into my car, and checking your pulse, and he came here to help me get you into bed...I am truly sorry, Tom, I've never done anything like that before. I am really glad that you're okay!"

"Mr. Wilson?"

"Yes, he claimed to know you…he asked a lot of questions. He seemed very concerned." Sophia lay back on the bed and turned to face me. "Do you know him?' She asked.

"Yes. At least I know of him. Apparently he was my father's…Jack Forsome's assistant."

"He said to tell you that he'd check back on you today," she said.

She lay on the bed inches away from me, large brown eyes fixed on me, her hair a blonde shambles, smeared make-up. At this point, I sort of lost track of the conversation. She wasn't beautiful, but she was attractive. A wild idea came to me. I should kiss her.

I was frozen with indecision. I think she noticed because her eyes got bigger, softer; and she got just a little funny kind of smile. Neither of us moved. A long time seemed to go by.

Then a voice from another room: "Mom! I'm off to school! See ya later!" A door banged somewhere.

The spell was broken. The electricity faded. Sophia jumped up from the bed. "That was my son, Robert. Robbie," She explained apologetically. "He's eleven and he's very self-sufficient."

"Oh," I said. I thought 'is there also a husband around?'

She went on, "You should know, I'm not married. I made a mistake, a wrong boyfriend, and I just couldn't do the abortion thing. I'm an unwed mother, just so you know, so if you want to...." She sort of lost her way. "Well, you know." She finished.

"I'm not a judgmental person," I said quickly. "People are going to be people. We often don't do the perfect thing."

"I didn't think you'd be the judgmental type, Tom. You seem very calm and accepting of things, to me. Nice to be around."

Typical of me, I just had no clue how to respond but her saying that made me feel warm. Lamely I came up with, "I imagine sometimes it's difficult being a parent by yourself."

"Actually I am so glad it happened, Robbie is a genuine happiness for me. Well, most times, anyway."

We were interrupted by a loud knock on the door.

Chapter 12: Deputy Somerville

Sophia's apartment turned out to be a neat little two-story, and we hustled down the stairs to the door in the living room, smoothing our clothes and hair on the way. I waited out of sight in the kitchen while Sophia checked the peephole.

"It's a cop!" she whispered in a frenzy. "What should we do?"

"Tell the truth. It'll be OK. Just tell the truth," I said, as if repeating it made it true.

She opened the door, "Yes?" she said.

"Hello miss, I'm Deputy Somerville of the Locust Area Police Department. Are you Miss Sophia Johnson?" A deep voice from outside.

"Yes I am. I'm Miss Johnson. How may I help you?"

"Well there was an incident reported yesterday and we have reason to believe you may have been involved. Do you mind answering a few questions so we can clear this up?"

"No, of course not. I mean, sure. Ask away."

"Do you mind if I step in for a moment?"

'Oh, no, please come in." She shut the door behind him. While I was listening I noticed a mug rack on the wall beside me. There were three blue mugs, three green mugs, and four red mugs, all in random order.

"Did you happen to be at Greendale, the Forsome Estate, yesterday afternoon, Miss Johnson?" the officer asked.

"Well, uh, yes. You see, I'm in real estate and the property may come up for sale and I was hoping for the listing," Sophia said. There was a nervous quality in her voice.

"Some people believe there may have been a shooting there yesterday afternoon. Did you witness a shooting?"

Calmly I rearranged the mugs: four red on the lower rungs, three green in the middle, and three blue on top. Everything in proper order. It made me feel a lot better.

"Oh, good heavens, no!" Sophia exclaimed. Her voice had become even more nervous. "Not that I saw. Was there a shooting?"

"We have no hard evidence that anything like that happened, although some witnesses are insisting,"

Deputy Somerville said. "But were you trespassing?" He asked.

Sophia stammered and I suspected she was having trouble finding a reasonable answer. So before she could recover I took a deep breath and stepped into the room. "Perhaps I can clear that up, officer," I said. "She was there legally, at my request."

Relief spread across Sophia's face like sunshine on a daffodil. Then it was replaced with concern as Deputy Somerville stiffened and demanded: "And who might you be, sir?"

"My name is Tom Palmer, and I was at the estate yesterday. I insisted that Miss Johnson join me there."

"Tom Palmer, I see." Deputy Somerville had become considerably more on edge. "We have some questions for you Mr. Palmer...Do you have a gun?"

"No, I've never owned a gun." I said. "Oh wait; I had a squirt gun with me yesterday. Is that what you mean?"

"A squirt gun? May I see it?"

Suddenly I realized I had no idea where the squirt gun or dark glasses had gotten to when I was tranquilized. And come to think of it, what was Deputy Somerville going to look like when I slipped on the glasses?

Sophia answered about the squirt gun: "Oh, I put it on the kitchen table last night."

Off we went to the kitchen.

I picked up the squirt gun and glasses. It struck me that I should put the glasses on, casually and inconspicuously, just in case.

"May I see the gun?" Deputy Somerville insisted. He reached out and I let him take it out of my hand while I fumbled clumsily with the glasses.

"Looks harmless enough," Deputy Somerville said, turning it over in his hand. "Does it shoot well?" Casually he hefted the squirt gun, and then aimed it at the kitchen sink.

I gasped aloud with dismay as he deftly squeezed the trigger. How would I explain the blue donut thingy?

A huge stream of water spurted from the gun and splashed impressively into the sink.

With astonished relief at the gun's output, I finally got the glasses onto my face and looked at Deputy Somerville. Thankfully he looked just like a normal guy, no bulging eyes or blue skin or anything like that.

And he was smiling now, saying, "I guess you didn't kill a man with this, did you?"

"No, I sure didn't kill a man with that, or with anything else." I agreed enthusiastically. "Come to think of it, I never saw a body or anything. Is there a body?"

"No, that's the funny thing. Your cousins claim you shot and killed one Special Deputy Underhill, who they say they met yesterday at the new McGregory's Fast Burgers next to the police station. But as far as we know there's no Special Deputy Underhill employed in any police department anywhere."

"So the man my cousins saw was a fraud?" I asked.

"We have no idea who he is, and there's no body. Your cousins point to a place near the cellar door as the spot where they claim the shooting took place, but there's no evidence of foul play that we could find." Deputy Somerville was considerably relaxed now.

"So what are you going to do now?" I asked.

"No body, no evidence, no crime. We have to drop it." He answered. "Oh, by the way, they claim you were trespassing but as I understand it, you might be as entitled to be there as they are, according to the papers."

"Well I didn't think I was trespassing," I agreed.

"I'd suggest you might avoid the place for the time being, though, just so as to not stir up any unnecessary trouble."

"That's good advice," I nodded agreeably.

He went on, "And we'd appreciate a phone number where you could be contacted in case other questions come up."

I was just wondering what had become of my cell phone during all of yesterday's excitement when Sophia stepped up. "Here, you can reach him at this number, most times." She gave him the number of her cell phone.

"Thanks. Well, that wraps up my questions," Deputy Somerville concluded. "Good day, Miss Johnson. Good day Mr. Palmer." With that he left.

The door closed behind him and Sophia practically jumped me. "That was wonderful, Tom!" She exclaimed. "I was sure he was going to arrest me for murder and then you stepped in took charge and just cleared it all up! Thank you sooo much! That was really marvelous of you." She grabbed my hand.

I noted that she could run on a bit sometimes, but I wasn't minding at all. "Well I don't think it was all that special," I said.

"Yes it was," she insisted. "You could have snuck out the back door and left me alone, but you didn't! I didn't know what I was going to do next. I was so nervous. Tom, you've earned a kiss for saving me!"

Here comes a peck on the cheek, I thought. It wasn't. It was a big long smackeroo right on the lips. It left me with the tingling feel of her lips, a sense of her warmth, the sweet female aroma of her, and the tickling of long blonde wisps of hair on my face. I don't often get that close to a woman and it all felt good.

"Oh my," she said, blushing, when it was over.

All I could get out was, "Your phone number. Why give him your phone number?"

"I don't know," she said. "I saw you were thinking and so I just did it."

"I couldn't remember what became of my phone."

"Oh, it's upstairs. I set it aside when I put you to bed." She giggled. "That sounds funny doesn't it?"

I laughed along with her. "I suppose I better give you my number in case they call you looking for me," I said.

We were exchanging phone numbers and addresses when she broke out laughing out loud. I didn't see anything funny, so I asked, "What?"

She pointed. "You rearranged my mugs!" she exclaimed.

We were laughing together when there was another knock on the door. I was getting tired of knocks on the door.

Locust Daily Register, May 24: According to Locust Police Department spokesman, Mr. and Mrs. Albert Brown and their two sons were reported missing after they failed to return from dinner at Phillip's All-U-Can-Eat Smorgasbord yesterday evening.

Chapter 13: Marty Again

Sophia went to the door while I stepped back into the kitchen, out of sight.

She peered through the peep hole. "It's Mr. Wilson," she whispered, and immediately opened the door.

Marty Wilson stood at the door. He was with a kid, who waved bye and ran off when the door opened. It wasn't one of the kids who had been with him yesterday.

Anyway, Marty Wilson walked right in, smiling nervously. "Good morning Miss Johnson."

"Good morning Mr. Wilson." She had a big smile for him, although somehow he still made me nervous.

"Is Tom Palmer still here?" he asked. I might have liked to hear a bit more, being unsure of his angle in all this, but Sophia said, "Yes, of course. He's in the kitchen."

I stepped into the living room. "Hi, nice to see you again," I said. I'm sure it sounded sincere.

"Good to see you again, too, how are you feeling this morning?" he asked.

"I seem to be doing fine, at least so far," I allowed.

He turned to Sophia, "I'm sorry, Miss Johnson, but I must speak with Mr. Palmer alone. Would you mind terribly if he and I stepped outside for a minute or two?"

Outside we walked half a block away from Sophia's house. She lived on a street lined with mature trees and a strip of grass on each side of the sidewalk. Small front yards, some with neat gardens.

Finally he exclaimed, "You opened the Vault! That means your DNA is true!"

"True to what?" I demanded.

"True to your father's. They chose him because his DNA was judged especially likely to succeed."

"Succeed at what, exactly?"

He looked around nervously. "You need to believe me about this, okay?" he pleaded.

"Believe what?"

"Your father was chosen to represent Earth to the Galactic Congress."

"My father represented the Earth with the Galactic Congress," I repeated.

"That's what I said," Marty Wilson agreed. "Have you used the gun and glasses yet?"

"I have some questions about the gun and glasses," I said. I was considering how much I wanted to tell him. Should I trust him? What is he after, I wondered.

Then a car door slammed loudly a half block further down the street from Sophia's house. We both turned to look. A tall bald man in a stern dark suit and serious shades was crossing the street, headed in our direction. I thought I had seen him before, but I didn't recall where right away.

"Dammit!" Exclaimed Marty Wilson. "Patricia can explain the gun and glasses." He took off in the opposite direction from the tall guy, at not quite a run. "And find your father's new will!" he called back to me.

I was tempted to start after him, but the tall guy called out "Hold it right there, Palmer!"

He had a deep authoritative voice.

"I see you've been talking to Martin Wilson, haven't you." He stated. It wasn't really a question.

"Well, yeah, I was."

"I am Agent Stewart Thorndyke, assigned to a special branch of the NSC." He announced. He flashed open his suit to reveal a garishly shiny badge hanging on his belt. Although for all I could see, he might have got it at Wal-Mart.

"Well, good for you." I said.

He either ignored or didn't notice my tone of voice, and went on, "My group's function is to quell baseless rumors which may cause stress and panic among the citizenry, specifically regarding spreading lies about aliens visiting the Earth. It is the official Policy of the United States Government that aliens do not exist. To differ with that policy is dangerous and unacceptable. Do you believe in aliens, Mr. Palmer?"

"Well, I'm a naturally skeptical person," I began.

He interrupted impatiently, before I got to the 'but' part of my thinking. "Good. Because if I thought you did believe in aliens, I have the authority to incarcerate you for a very long time."

"Uh, just suppose I actually see an alien, not that I really did, but what then? "

"We both know it's invariably a trick of the lighting, an optical illusion, every time. We agree that aliens do not exist. If you go around claiming to see aliens, we're going to have to put you away. It's that simple. By the way, we're close to picking up your friend Wilson, all we need is one more incident."

"Wow. I'll warn him to behave if I see him again."

Agent Thorndyke left me with a warning to be careful who I hang around with, and stay clean of panicking the populace with nonsense alien stories. Shaking my head, I returned to Sophia's to say goodbye.

She looked disappointed that I was leaving. "When will I see you again?" she asked.

I didn't have to think of an answer, it came all on its own. "Whenever you want," I replied.

"Oh, then how about dinner at the new McGregory's, downtown? I hear they have great burgers."

"Great. Shall I pick you up around 6:00?"

"That would be fine. Meanwhile, I have to run some errands this morning. Can I give you a ride somewhere?"

"Thanks, but no. My car is only a few blocks away, and I need to make a stop or two along the way."

Chapter 14: Confronting Attorney Smith.

Stop number one was Attorney Jonathon Smith, Esquire. What he said to me yesterday wasn't jiving with what I'd been hearing from others.

"Oh, Mr. Palmer. How nice to see you again. How may we help?" Smith's secretary was less than enthused.

"May I speak to Mr. Smith, please. I'm afraid some things we discussed yesterday weren't exactly clear."

"Please have a seat and I'll see if he's available." She went off down the hall. I decided to look around a bit rather than sit. The nameplate on her desk said 'Mrs. Maude Goehring. Before I discovered anything else beyond out of date issues of Sports Illustrated and People Magazine, she was back, along with Smith.

"Mr. Palmer, Mr. Palmer!" exclaimed Smith. "How are you today? It's so good of you to drop by. How can we help you today?"

"Uh, perhaps we could talk privately..."

"Of course." He led the way into his office. We sat, across the huge desk from each other.

"What's on your mind? You seem a bit perturbed today. Is everything OK?" Smith was exceedingly polite and solicitous.

 "Well I'd like to clarify a thing or two from yesterday's discussion," I started, "Apparently you are not executer of Jack Forsome's will."

"Which will?" he asked. "You see, the earlier will has been registered, naming Troy Conners as executor, but there is a later will which has not yet been located, and which will take precedence once it is properly processed."

"How do you know this?"

"I have been in contact with a Mr. Marty Wilson, who was associated with your father. I prepared a draft of a new will for your father's approval, according to his instructions, and Wilson took it to Dr. Forsome. Apparently Dr. Forsome signed it before witnesses, but then he neglected to provide me with a copy. "

"What did it say?"

"It was done long enough ago that I can't recall precisely, so instead of guessing at specifics I'd rather not risk getting the details wrong."

"You got all this information from Marty Wilson?"

"Mr. Wilson has been very helpful. It was he of course who brought the fact of your parentage to me, some months ago."

"The fact of my parentage."

"Yes, you are definitely Jack Forsome's son. The DNA tests are quite reliable regarding paternity issues."

"My cousins plan to ignore me and my DNA."

"Of course they do. Which is why you must locate the new will, and you must confirm your DNA analysis. They will then be required to give you due consideration."

"And if the will names me, I stand to inherit everything?"

"Probably. There may be bequests and such."

"By the way, are you aware that Marty Wilson claims to be involved with aliens?"

"If he is, that would be his business, not mine. Personally, I know nothing of aliens. In fact, alien stories and rumors – abductions and such - are mostly just the attempts of sad and unimportant people trying to bolster their self-importance."

Did I forget any key questions? I don't think so, so I left. But Marty Wilson seemed to keep turning up. On impulse I checked my cell phone, and found his number from when he had called me, yesterday. I pressed the call button.

"Wilson."

"Palmer."

"Yes. Sorry I had to run off like that this morning, I uh, had an appointment to keep."

"I have some questions for you."

"I'm not surprised. I can meet you at the Rose & Thorn Pub in a half hour."

I was sipping a Bloody Mary when Marty Wilson arrived, ten minutes late.

"Hello," he said. "This must all be very disorienting for you."

"Very." I admitted. "So I had a nice discussion with your friend agent Thorndyke after you left this morning."

"I'll bet. What did he have to say?"

"That he's with the NSC. That he's about to arrest you for treason or something, all to do with aliens."

Wilson laughed. "That's funny. We used to work together, with your father. He provided security when needed. He's a rent-a-cop these days. I think he was hired by your cousins to keep you and me away from their opportunity to cash in on your father's estate."

"He's not a federal agent?"

"Not a chance."

"Why are you avoiding him?"

He shrugged. "I lost a bet. I owe him a hundred dollars. I don't want to pay him."

"What about all the alien nonsense you keep pushing? It seems pretty off base, doesn't it?"

He sighed. "I guess you'll have to decide about aliens for yourself. Just remember, the little green men are not your friends."

After he left, I looked up IdentityDNA.com on an impulse. I discovered the Locust division of the General Hospital happened to have a branch, only a dozen or so blocks away. I stopped by, showed identification, and they took a swab. I asked for the results promptly, certified for court use, and they promised tomorrow morning. They wanted $259.59! I was astonished, but under the circumstances I decided I'd better pay up. Bloodsuckers. Well, spitsuckers, anyway.

On the way back to my Honda, my iPhone rang.

"Palmer."

"Conners. Troy Conners."

"Oh, hello, cousin Troy. What can I do for you?"

"We gotta talk. Meet us at the Rose & Thorn, half an hour."

"What do we gotta talk about?"

"Just be there! Half an hour!" Click.

Still real friendly. I tossed a mental coin to decide whether I would meet them or not, and I lost the toss: I'd go see what they wanted.

Troy and Larry were waiting at a table in the back corner. Troy waved, motioning me to a chair across from the two of them. I sat, and the bartender came over.

"Hi Troy. Hi Larry. Having the usual?" He asked.

"Yeah the usual, all around. " The bartender left and we eyed each other warily across the table.

The usual turned out to be Coors Light. Larry took a huge swill from his glass, collecting foam around his mouth. He let out a hearty belch, and wiped his mouth with his sleeve. "This is real beer," he announced proudly, holding up his glass. "They make it with fresh mountain water, you know."

"Yeah, so I've heard." What else could I say to that?

Troy leaned forward like he was going to let me in on a secret. "We're gonna give you an opportunity, Palmer. If you're smart, you'll take it."

"Okay, what's the deal?"

'First we pay you $5,000 dollars. Then we give you 2% of the business venture we have planned with Uncle Jack's estate. Then you go away and forget all about Jack Forsome."

"Business venture? What's that?" I asked.

"A Sports Bar," Larry blurted. "We're gonna build the Greendale Sports Bar!"

"Shut up, Larry!" Troy yelled. "That's a secret, remember?"

"Oh, yeah. Well maybe it ain't gonna be a sports bar."

"How about it, Palmer? It's a good deal, you make out financially and you avoid a bunch of headaches. Just think: $5,000 and 2%!"

I wasn't sure they could be taken seriously. So I temporized. "Well. I certainly appreciate the offer. Let me think on it." I told them.

Troy wrote his iPhone number on the napkin Larry hadn't used. He slid it carefully across the table at me. "Here's my cell number. Call me anytime. We'll have the cash ready," he assured me. That concluded our business. Larry finished his Coors Light, belched again and they left.

After that, I decided it was time to go home for a nap, and let all the nonsense sort itself out while I slept.

Your Local Locust Metro Newscast, Noon May 24: Several witnesses who observed an unusual flash of light in the sky yesterday were told by authorities that a rare cloud formation caught in sunlight is the most likely explanation for the phenomenon. Regarding reports of a flying saucer, authorities said succinctly, 'Yeah, right. Remember they saw it just after Happy Hour.'

Chapter 15: McGregory's

I dropped by Sophia's house and when no one answered the door, I decided to let myself in. The door was unlocked. The downstairs was empty and after some hesitation, I went up the steps. I heard a noise in the bedroom, so I called "Hello? It's me, Tom Palmer." I opened the door.

Sophia stood by the bed, wearing only a bath towel, carefully wrapped. "Hello Tom," she smiled at me. "I was hoping you'd visit. I have a question; I hope you don't think it too personal."

"No, it's okay. Ask away."

"Are you in a relationship? I mean is there someone you're ...well, romantically involved with?"

I shook my head. "No, I'm unconnected."

"Me too," Sophia declared. She dropped the towel. "Let's make love," she whispered huskily.

Then I awoke with a start. I was in my own bed, napping. Alone. Dreaming. Dammit.

Back in the real world, I tried to collect my thoughts with a reheated cup of stale coffee.

Here I was, torn out of my normally quiet and calm existence into some madcap escapade where I seemed to be tossed about by events basically out of my control. And usually I am a person who likes to manage my life for myself.

The unavoidable fact was I didn't really have any compelling reason to believe, or to not believe, anybody I'd met in the last two days. Therefore:

I was no longer sure who my father was.

I might be in line to inherit an undefined large sum.

I may have had alien encounters.

The only thing I was sure of was that I wanted to see Sophia again. Fortunately, I had a date with her. I decided I'd try to ignore the other stuff and see how things turn out.

I dropped by Sophia's house at 6. She invited me in for a drink before we went to dinner. She opened a bottle of Merlot, a dark red wine when poured in the glasses.

We sat in the living room and chatted. She laughed at my jokes, I laughed at hers. She laughed a lot. I liked that about her. I asked about Robbie, her son.

He was a good kid. Tonight, he was sleeping over at her cousin's place, on the other side of town.

Finally she said, "Here's the dirty little secret from my past. I met Craig while I was in college. I thought we were the real thing, but somehow we never got around to a wedding ceremony, and then suddenly Craig decided to go off to Portland with his friends."

"Why would he do that?" I asked.

"I'm not sure; I think it was just wanderlust, at first. I followed him to Portland, but Portland is cold and wet. The worst of it is, Craig came under the influence of a group of survivalists. He changed into a completely different person, a mean and hostile person."

"Something frightened him?"

"That's what I thought. All he wanted to do was throw everything we had into building a bunker deep in the woods, in preparation for the coming cataclysm. Him and his big guard dogs! He made those dogs mean, too."

"Therefore the tranquilizer gun."

"Yeah, those mastiffs frightened me. No conspiracy theory was too crazy for Craig: Jews, Moslems,

Mexicans, Russians, Big Business. His favorite was evil aliens...it seemed everybody was out to get him. I became an expert alien debunker, but no matter what I said, it was like water off a duck's back."

"Paranoia?"

"I suppose it was. Finally I realized he wasn't going to get any better. It was no situation to be raising Robbie in, so I came back here and moved in with my parents for a few years. Then, a couple years ago, they moved to North Carolina to escape the cold winters, and I've been on my own since then."

"I can see how you had to get out of the situation in Oregon." I said.

"And you?" She asked. "You seem to be highly eligible. You're not attached?"

"I was once, but not anymore. Her name is Zelda. We met when I saw her perform at the local theatre. She was friendly, intelligent, funny, pretty, and ambitious."

"Sounds perfect."

"I thought so. We spent a lot of time together and I thought we were getting serious, but then she landed a couple of nice parts in a show in NYC, and she left town without even bothering to tell me."

"That's really a selfish thing to do."

"Yeah. We were in touch for a while, until she got an offer on the west coast and off she went. Meanwhile I discovered she had been very friendly with more guys than just me, so with that it was over. We still talk now and then, but I realize she'll never be exclusive, and she'll never leave show business."

"Would you go to her if she asked?"

"No. We're through. I finally realized that she just isn't the kind to marry and settle down."

Funny, the bottle of Merlot was empty. We decided it was time to go eat. Since her place was just three blocks from the restaurant, we decided to walk.

McGregory's was bright and clean, trimmed in a blue and white motif featuring cute little flowers. There was lots of lighting in the ceiling, making the place perhaps a bit too bright. The layout featured a counter where you ordered, and a couple of dining rooms. Servers brought the food to your table when it was ready. There were only a couple of empty tables in the main dining room.

"I hear this place is owned and operated by an immigrant family from someplace in Asia," Sophia commented as we were shown to our seats in the main dining room. The people who came in after us, a large older couple, were shown into the other dining room. The server shut the door after them.

I looked around. The guys at the cash register and ordering counter looked swarthy, and were only about 5' tall. The two ladies delivering food had dark hair tied in thick buns, and were even shorter than the cash register guy. The busboy was shorter yet.

"I suppose that's why they're all uniformly short," I noted.

Sophia put on a pair of fashionable reading glasses to review the menu. "I like burgers so that's probably what I'll have," she said, "But I want to see what else is on the menu."

"Nice glasses, they complement your face," I said. She looked really nice tonight. Somehow, I managed to say so: "You look really nice, Sophia."

She smiled. "Thank you, Tom. But my glasses are nowhere as cool as your blue sunglasses."

"Oh yeah, they're something." I got them out of my pocket. "And they fit really well, too."

Casually I slipped them on to see if they'd cut the glare.

Sophia was tinted slightly blue, seen through the blue mirror lenses. "You look especially nice in a light shade of blue," I said. I looked around to see if the rest of the place was tinted blue, too.

I glanced at the register. Seen through the sunglasses, the guy there was a short green creature with large pointy ears and no nostrils. His eyes were bulging black blobs protruding from his face. As he handed a credit card back to a paying customer, I saw his hands had long spindly green fingers with claw-like nails.

I blinked in astonishment. The thing looked like a goblin straight out of World of Warcraft, but meaner. I took the glasses off, and he looked like a short swarthy guy from Asia. I put the glasses back on and he was definitely a little green creature – a goblin. Then I saw that the server ladies, the busboy and the order taker were also goblins. Suddenly I was very nervous. I'd heard bad things about these buggers, but I didn't recall where I'd heard it. Something else: I realized there was a slight aroma to the air, vaguely reminiscent of skunk cabbage.

I noticed the door to the other dining room had swung open briefly. The light seemed to be really bright in there. I didn't see the couple who had just been seated there. Where did they go, that fast, I wondered. They were both quite large and should have been easy to spot. Then a goblin in the other room grabbed the door and shut it firmly. Somehow the way he did it was chillingly ominous.

I had really bad vibes. I took a deep breath and reminded myself: I don't believe in bad vibes. I still had really bad vibes, anyway. "We've got to get out of here," I said hoarsely.

"What? We just got here. Aren't you hungry?" Sophia looked at me with concern.

"We've got to get out of here." I repeated. "We can eat somewhere else. Let's go," I insisted, sliding out of my chair. The goblins were acting just like normal people, serving food and busing tables. But they had no mouths, which was really freaky.

Sophia was staring at me with surprise. "Are you okay? The menu isn't *that* bad," she protested.

"It's the glare," I said lamely. "It's hurting my eyes." The goblin at the register was looking at us. It turned as if saying something to the order taker, who then looked directly at me. But they had no mouths. I could only tell that it was talking because the skin where the mouth should be was wiggling. Both goblins glanced toward the other room, then back at me.

Suddenly I knew what had become of the other couple. I recalled reading stories of people disappearing in the Locust Shopping News.

"We need to leave *now*," I insisted. I took Sophia's hand to help her out of her seat. Perhaps I was a little urgent about it.

"Tom, you're making a scene," she protested as I hurried her out the front door.

"I'm sorry, but we had to get out of there. We're in danger here." I said, as we reached the sidewalk outside. I guess I sounded pretty desperate. Well, I was feeling pretty desperate. Here I had always known there were no aliens, but here they were, right in downtown Locust, PA.

Sophia stopped on the sidewalk, looking at me with a funny expression. "What has come over you?" she asked. "That seemed uncalled for."

Three of the goblins had come to the front window, looking out at us. One pointed at me, and said something to the others. Wiggle, wiggle, wiggle; little mouth spot.

Before I could stop myself I pointed at them and blurted, "They're not from Asia, they're aliens. They're goblins - little green men from Alpha Centari or someplace!"

Sophia's face turned dark with shock and disappointment.

Quickly I took off the glasses and handed them to Sophia. "Here, look for yourself."

She put the glasses on, turned, and looked carefully into McGregory's front window, right at the Goblins. She took the glasses off and handed them back to me, shaking her head.

"They're just people from Asia," she said.

"What?" I put the glasses on. I saw little green men. "You don't see aliens?"

"No I don't, Tom. This stuff about aliens is very disturbing nonsense," Sophia declared. "I had my fill of stupid conspiracy stories, including aliens, before, and I don't need anymore. Do you really believe you're seeing little green men?"

There they were, staring at me through McGregory's front window. Now there were six of them. I could see they were talking, even though they had no mouths, because the spot where their mouths should be was going squiggle, squiggle, and squiggle. Disgusting!

I was on the spot. What could I say?   Nothing came to mind. Finally I said, "Uh…."

Sophia sighed and said, "I'm sorry. I don't think this is going to work. I just can't deal with another crazy. Goodbye, Tom." She left and I could only watch her walk away.

Chapter 16: Backyard Battle

I was crushed. I looked back at the goblins. One was talking into a thing in its hand that looked like a cell phone. I wondered who it might be calling.

Clearly I needed more information. I remembered: Marty Wilson had warned me about little green men. I went to my car and called.

"Wilson."

"Palmer"

"I expected you might call."

"I'll bet. What do you know about little green men?"

"Pointy ears, antennae, buggy eyes, and the freaky part: no visible mouth."

"What are they after? How many are there?"

"I take it you've seen them."

"Yeah, I've seen them."

"Okay. I'll meet you at the Rose and Thorn, half an hour." The Rose and Thorn was getting to be a habit.

He was on time, this time. We sat at the bar. The bartender said to me, "Nice to see you again, sir. Bloody Mary? Or, Coors Light?"

Definitely the Bloody Mary.

"Okay what are they after?" I confronted Marty Wilson.

"What they're after, I'm afraid, is you."

"Why would they be after me? Oh, I get it, my DNA, right?"

"Bingo." He nodded.

"I'm not buying into this. I think I'm outta here. I don't need money. I like my quiet life, with lots of crossword activity. "

"You can't do that!" He was upset.

"Why not? My cousins offered me cash to go away...I just might take them up on it."

"Don't. Let me give you three reasons. First, your cousins have no money. They hired Thorndyke for $1000 a day to guard Greendale, then only paid him $100. The rest is contingent, they said."

I had to laugh. "I'm not surprised. What else?"

"Second, the children."

"What do you mean, the children.

"We run a foundation which supports carefully selected children until they complete a college education. Due to Dr. Forsome's death, the funding has stopped. You need to reinstate funding to the foundation."

"You mean like orphans? How many children?"

"Some are Orphans. We now have 35 kids in various stages of the program."

"So you're telling me these kids depend on me or they go back to starvation or something like that?"

"Maybe not quite that dire, but yes. We're very concerned for the children. I was reluctant to load this on you too soon."

"Thanks a lot. What's the third reason."

He looked guilty. "You have to save Earth from the alien invasion. "

"Back to that! What's with that?'

"You're going to need all the details. You need to go see Patricia for that."

So that was next: visiting Patricia at the Interstellar Communication Center. The only way I knew to get there was the TeeDee, so I made my way to

Greendale, the Forsome property, and snuck through the hole in the fence.

When I reached the backyard I snuck along the bushes toward the house. Luckily I spotted Stewart Thorndyke, pacing near the barbeque pit. Another strange character who's given me a lame story, I thought. I was in a foul, confrontational mood, so I snuck up and jumped out at him.

"Hey! Seen any aliens?" I yelled.

I startled him thoroughly. He jumped about three feet off the ground.

"Palmer! What do you think you're doing here?" he demanded.

"Just out for a stroll," I said. "How about you...here on NSC business, are you?"

"I guess you found out that was an act, huh."

"Yeah."

"Your cousins scripted that. It was supposed to scare you off, keep you out of their way, that's all."

"So you are on my cousin's payroll. The script didn't work."

"Yeah, well, they stiffed me. I'd quit but then they wouldn't pay me what they already owe me. By the way, I'm supposed to call them if you show up here. Mind if I do that?"

"No, go right ahead. But I won't be here when they arrive."

Thorndyke looked up and did a classic double take. He craned his neck staring up. "You really should leave right now. There's strange things' going on here." He warned.

"Like what...aliens?"

"Ha ha. Put on your glasses." He pointed up. I saw nothing with a quick glance upward.

Then I noticed he wore glasses with blue mirror lenses, just like the ones I'd gotten from Marty Wilson. I fumbled mine out of my pocket and onto my face and looked up.

There was a flying saucer just overhead. Christmas lights danced around its outer edge.

A hole opened like a sphincter, centered on the saucer's belly. A big white shiny blob of something fell out of the hole. It looked like a huge snowball except for the red and black highlights shimmering on it. It looked almost alive. As it fell gently to the ground, another blob fell out of the saucer, then another.

The first blob landed at the far end of the backyard, 50 or so yards away. It seemed to sort of evaporate, revealing an insect that stood about six feet tall. The insect had a triangular face, with twitching antennas atop and mandibles drooping below. Compound eyes bulged from the upper corners of the triangular face, like bulbous radar domes. The head sat on a chest-sized thorax which sprouted six legs and complex wings. A pointy-ended abdomen trailed behind the thing. It was mostly black, with streaks of red.

The thing's head swiveled this way and that, then centered on Thorndyke and I. Meanwhile the other two blobs landed near the first, and out popped two additional monstrosities, more or less identical to the first.

"I'm going to take care of these beauties," snarled Thorndyke. He whipped a pistol from under his jacket, and set off marching determinedly toward the aliens as he cocked the gun.

I thought, 'he must be completely insane', but I got out my squirt gun, reluctantly. I started after

Thorndyke but more slowly. Much more slowly. Unfortunately I managed to trip over the edge of the patio and sprawled face first onto the grass. I hung onto the squirt gun, but the glasses leapt off my head and caromed away beneath the nearby bushes.

Prone, I looked up to see Thorndyke marching onward with blazing gun. The gun went Pfft, pfft, pfft – I guessed he had a silencer. It didn't stop the insects, which were now advancing on him. They each had a gun-like thing that shot a red laser beam at Thorndyke, but the beams just dissipated around him, as if he wore a suit of body armor. The glasses? I wondered.

I looked around for my glasses and suddenly realized I could see the aliens without them. These big bugs apparently didn't bother with disguises. But looking up, I couldn't see the saucer...it was evidently cloaked. I spotted my glasses where they had skittered behind a bush, and I crawled under the bush to retrieve them. I grabbed them and turned to peer through the bush at the action in the backyard.

Thorndyke had stopped halfway down the yard and was still blasting away. One of the bugs finally collapsed in a heap but then the other two reached him. One grabbed and lifted him like a baby, and the other swiftly jabbed him with the pointy end of its abdomen. "Stinger", I thought. Thorndyke went limp almost immediately, dropping his gun.

One Alien said to the other: <pop, whistle, beep, click, buzz.> Anyway, that's what I heard it say. I also heard a translation, softly spoken in my ear: it had said, <What about the other creature?>

The other alien responded: <beep, whistle, buzz, click, ding.> It meant, <I do not see it. We have the creature with the disruption glasses. That is the one Prime Sister wants. We cannot be faulted.>

Just then a car came down the driveway toward the house. A red Toyota. 'Oh no!' I thought. The aliens with Thorndyke shrank into shadows among the bushes. When the car got to the middle of the driveway a wide golden beam of light speared down from the saucer and engulfed the car. The car stopped.

The driver's door opened and Sophia got out of the car, spotlighted by the beam from the saucer. Her hair stood straight up as if she were in a big time updraft. In a trance, she sleep-walked directly at the insect monsters, who met her halfway across the backyard, carrying Thorndyke, right beside the bug that had fallen. All gathered, the beam of light centered on the group. "Sophia!" I yelled but she paid no attention.

I scrambled to my feet and started running at them. Too late! Just like in a Spielberg movie they all rose swiftly up the beam of light and disappeared into the saucer. The hole in its belly slid shut. I stopped running and aimed my squirt gun at it, but I stopped just before pulling the trigger – What if I shot and transformed it all into a huge puddle of water, including Sophia and Thorndyke?

Helpless, alone in the backyard, I watched as the saucer accelerated rapidly west and upward into the evening sky. Then it was gone.

Chapter 17: Pinco F-1 Again

I was stunned. Things had changed. Before I'd taken all these strange events sort of casually, like a minor irritation.   Now, things had become serious and I needed to be committed. And not to an asylum, but to figuring out what's going on.

From the backyard, I was into the house, into the vault, and into the helicopter...the TeeDee, in less than a minute, on my way to get help from Patricia. I found her as before, laying face up under a sheet, a cable stuck in her belly button.

The door did its ding dong thing when I entered. Patricia immediately sat up and looked at me. "You appear to be significantly agitated, Tom Palmer." She observed.

"Damn right! They kidnapped Sophia!   And Thorndyke." I almost exploded at her.

"If you calm down we will be able to exchange information much more efficiently." She advised. "Now please, who did what to whom?"

"These Big Black Bugs beamed Sophia and Thorndyke into their saucer and took off," I sputtered.

"Ant-like creatures with triangular heads?   And Red streaks all over?" She questioned.

"Yes."

"They were Krylki Sisters. But I expect they would have been after you. Why did they take the others and not you?"

"I think they *were* after me. I think they mistook Thorndyke for me. He had a pair of glasses like these." I showed her the glasses. "But why would they be after me? And just what are these glasses?"

"They are after you because you are the terrestrial representative to the Galactic Congress, and therefore you have the ability to disrupt their plans for harvesting this planet's resources." She explained.

I was still trying to absorb that when she went on, "The glasses are Disruption Lenses. They provide a force field surrounding you that monitors incoming particles and prohibits unwanted ones. For example, both the Krylki weapons and the various disguise generators utilized by them and their subordinates operate through particle driven forces and are therefore disrupted harmlessly."

"Let's go back to the galactic congress thing. Why me?" This had bugged me ever since this unbelievable sequence of events had begun. I'd never been anyone special.

"Your DNA has been determined to create a superior likelihood of successfully carrying out the functions of a terrestrial representative."

"I'm not sure I understand what you mean by that."

"The Galactic Policy Board has analyzed all terrestrial DNA samples available, and has concluded that the makeup of your DNA indicates that you will decide and act more correctly than anyone else."

"I don't see how that's very likely. Lots of people are smarter than I am."

"The DNA analysis is sophisticated well beyond the capabilities of terrestrial science, and has been proven correct at numerous other locations. It is your destiny, Tom Palmer."

"Well, I guess that's really swell." I was thinking, 'so, some alien super brain has fingered me as the patsy. I suspect the selection is purely random, with a fancy explanation to sucker the poor klutz in.' "But right now I just want to get Sophia back," I went on. "And Thorndyke, I guess. And by the way, Marty Wilson said to ask you about my father's will."

"Your Father's will is in a safety deposit box owned jointly by your father and his sister, your Aunt Sally. She has probably forgotten to mention it. I understand she's been forgetting rather often. And I believe your objective to rescue Sophia is essentially consistent with your current assignments from Skudas Dorval."

"What assignments?"

"I tried to explain when you were here before, but you were not ready," She pointed out. "As I said before, you are to disrupt the Krylki plans to exploit Earth's resources."

"What resources are they planning to exploit?"

Patricia looked a bit uneasy at that. "I understand they plan to harvest protein."

"What protein?"

She hesitated a moment. "Homo Sapiens," she said finally.

I was a little slow here. "What do you mean, Homo Sapiens?"

"They utilize a complex food processor to convert Homo Sapiens specimens into an exceedingly nourishing and tasty form of food utilized by all three life stages of the Krylki." I looked at her blankly, not quite believing yet, and she added, "Would you like to see a sample?"

Speechlessly I nodded.

She opened a nearby cabinet and took out a Tupperware container. Well, that's what it looked like. She opened it and got out the object inside, holding it up for me to see.

It was a Girl Scout cookie. Chocolate Mint, in fact.

"Would you like a bite?" Patricia asked.

I nearly choked. "I will never ever again eat a Girl Scout chocolate mint cookie."

Patricia caught onto my body language, I think, and reassured me: "These are not Girl Scout cookies. Notice the Krylki symbol on the wafer." She pointed to a seven pointed starburst symbol, drawn with white icing on the cookies' underside. "They place this symbol on all their manufactured goods."

She returned the container to the cabinet and returned to me. "Back to your assignments. You must penetrate a Krylki infestation on your planets' surface. There you must procure information enabling you to find, infiltrate, and reprogram the Krylki Mothership."

"A Mothership, no less. How did they get here? I always heard that distances in the Universe are far too large to allow interstellar travel."

"That is true when your technology is limited by the speed of light. Several species have developed technology that allows them to achieve speeds well above light speed."

"And the Krylki have it."

"They utilize Zumola engines, reducing flight times to mere years instead of centuries. And they can readily endure hibernation for years at a time."

"About this infestation on the ground that we need to find. Are the little green men and the big blue things working with the Krylki?" I had a suspicion.

"Yes, green Goblins and blue Reptilicons. They are cloned creatures bred for servitude to the Krylki. Are you aware of an infestation involving them, on the planet's surface?"

"I certainly am," I said. I definitely knew of an infestation, right there in downtown Locust, PA. McGregory's Fast Burgers.

"The GPB prohibits ground occupation on preserved planets such as Earth," Patricia said. "Accordingly we are permitted to exterminate the infestation. As Galactic Representative, you have the authority to initiate and carry out such an action, with my assistance. Shall we proceed?"

"Is it necessary in order to rescue Sophia?"

"Yes."

"Let's do it."

It turns out the TeeDee had room for the two of us, though it was a bit close. For the occasion, Patricia had changed into a formfitting tunic and legging thing that, despite my growing suspicions about what she was, certainly displayed very human characteristics.

By now it was night and Emma flew the TeeDee close to the ground as we zoomed toward downtown Locust. As we went, I got out the squirt gun and showed it to Patricia. "Just what is this tricky little toy," I asked.

"It's a Toradex – a torus-emitting extermination device. The forces carried by the torus reduce the target's molecules to water. That is very convenient, when you don't want any evidence remaining." She explained.

"But it squirts water," I pointed out.

"Of course, and it is an excellently designed squirt gun, at that. Your father was quite proud of the design. The higher level functions only operate when empowered by a specific individual's DNA. Thus this particular model," she handed the gun back to me, "requires your DNA to operate fully."

"Deputy Somerville fired water from this into the kitchen sink. What if I had fired the gun instead of him?"

"You would have pulverized the kitchen sink," she explained calmly. "Note that there is a dial at the base of the handle. That selects the character of the forces emitted by the Toradex. The default white indicator elects just water. The green is for many small targets, the blue is for mid-sized, the black is for large, and the red, for huge, such as flying saucers. The yellow merely disables the target's movement temporarily. I expect you should set it on green for tonight's use."

"This can shoot down a flying saucer?" I was incredulous. I flipped the little dial to the green setting.

"Yes, but beware that that would draw down the toradex's power completely, to zero. It would not operate again until reloaded."

"What do you reload a thing like this with?"

"Refill it with water. It uses water to generate its power."

"How can it do that?" I was quickly sorry I had asked.

Patricia said, "The toroidal shape used is similar to a doughnut but rather than having an empty central "hole", the topology of the torus folds in upon itself and all points along its surface converge together into a zero-dimensional point at the center called the Vertex. This makes it the perfect environment within which to populate the automatous partials that make up the essence of any dynamic function such as a person's vibrational essence. Any input placed at the Vertex while the torus is "torsioned" (folded and rotated inward) is spread out and distributed over the entire surface of the toroid, therefore converting the prior material configuration into a simple hydrogen/oxygen compound." Patricia said all this in a flat monotone, as if she were reading an encyclopedia entry found somewhere deep in her head.

I swear I considered this carefully, but summed up my conclusion: "That sounds like hocus-pocus gobble-de-gook nonsense to me. What does it mean in English?" Some of Patricia's explanations clearly required simplification.

"The Torus shape delivers and applies the forces which convert a creature's material being into water."

"So, basically, Zapp-o, Splash-o! Right?'

"That will work." She said dryly.

Chapter 18: The Raid

We arrived at McGregory's conveniently just after the 10 pm closing. All the customers had cleared out. We decided the back door would be the most effective entry point.

As I was a novice at this I let Patricia take the lead. I figured she would use some clever galactic subterfuge to sneak in, get what we needed and get out, with little if any conflict. Wrong.

"You first," I told her, indicating the door. I noticed she had a cute sneaky little smile I hadn't seen before. "Put on your glasses," she suggested.

As I settled the glassed on my nose, Patricia stepped up to the McGregory's backdoor and bashed it in with a ferocious kick. The door smashed onto the floor of the room inside with a huge crash. Without hesitation Patricia leapt through the doorway and into the room, like wonder woman on the attack.

It was a large storeroom, and it seemed to be filled with thoroughly surprised little green men. Just like a mob of goblins. At least ten of them, maybe fifteen, I thought with dismay. I noted two swinging doors left and right, leading out of the room.

Patricia landed upright on the fallen backdoor, feet braced, swinging her arms this way and that. Bright green donuts burst from her hands and splat went this goblin, then splat went that one over there, and splat, yet another. Water flew splashing about the room like a bucket fight at the local firehouse. Then the goblins had recovered from their surprise. Some drew weapons and fired on Patricia, while others fled through both of the swinging doors out of the room.

Bolts of light from the alien's weapons burst brilliantly around Patricia without effect, flaring like the strobe lights in a disco club. I leaned into the doorway and selected one of the ones shooting at Patricia, aimed, and squeezed the trigger. A green donut burst out and enveloped the thing, which promptly exploded into a flood of water. Meanwhile Patricia had disposed of three or four more. One last goblin remained, firing futilely at Patricia while trying to back out of the room through the door to the right.

"Dispose of that one," Patricia ordered, indicating the last one. Then she barged through the swinging door to the left, and into the main dining room. I saw more goblins there, as the door swung shut, but I focused on the last one in the storeroom: Zapp-o, Splash-o! The room was saturated with water.

I edged cautiously into the storeroom. The door to the dining area had swung shut behind Patricia. I could hear splashing water, while bursts of light shone intermittently around the door's edges.

I was looking around, wondering what we needed to find, when the door other than the one Patricia went through swung open. A man-sized black and red insect surged through, its' triangular head bobbing, confronting me. Its eyes sparkled angrily, if you can imagine such a thing of compound eyes.

I was quick at the trigger. A green donut surged onto the alien but merely slowed the thing momentarily. The squirt gun was on the wrong setting! Desperately I fumbled at the dial. As I did a second big black bug entered the room.

The first bug said <click, beep, whistle, buzz, dingdong,> which meant, <now we have you, pitiful specimen. I shall present your limp carcass to Prime Sister myself!>

It leapt on me and I fell flat on my back, the thing hanging over me maliciously. Its mandibles closed in on my face just as I switched the dial on my gun. I shoved the gun into the thing's squirming mushy mouth parts and pulled the trigger. It exploded into a bathtub full of water that nearly drowned me.

I was still coughing water out of my windpipes when the second bug knocked the squirt gun out of my hand and across the room. Before I could scramble off my back it was on me, all six limbs pinning me more securely than a moth in a bug collection. It flexed its stinger into readiness and prepared to skewer me with it. I couldn't break its hold no matter how hard I squirmed.

Just as its stinger began its downward motion to stab into my abdomen, Patricia burst through the door and hit the bug like an all-pro linebacker welcoming a rookie running back into the NFL. I could hear the carapace crunch where she impacted with the thing's thorax. Patricia was clearly a lot harder than she appeared. They crashed into the wall and I heard more crunching. Both of them appeared stunned by the collision.

I scrambled across the floor and retrieved the squirt gun. I turned and the bug had recovered before Patricia and was coming, albeit limping now, at me, stinger thrusting forward. Desperately I squeezed the trigger just before the stinger got me. Again I was saturated with a cascade of water as the bug disintegrated. I didn't mind.

I was still coughing out water as Patricia recovered. "Are you damaged, Tom Palmer? She asked. I had suspected she was an unfeeling android, but I knew I heard genuine concern in her voice.

"I think I'm OK," I managed. "How about you?"

"I shall repair promptly. I apologize; I should have anticipated the Sisters' presence here."

"I guess we prevailed anyway," I said.

"Yes we have." She pronounced. "And look. I have procured the information device we require for the next step." She held up a thumb drive just like the ones I stored my photos on.

I groaned. I was getting tired of ordinary objects turning out to be very unordinary.

Chapter 19: Making Plans

We discussed the next step while riding the TeeDee back to the Pinco F-1.

"Next we go get the Mothership and exterminate those aliens, right?" I opined.

"Approximately. The next step must be performed in compliance with the non-intervention policies laid out by the Galactic Congress, as administered by the GPB." Patricia warned.

I sighed. "Now what does that mean this time?"

"First, I can only assist to the full extent of my abilities while enforcing Board policies on ground infestations, since that is considered to be an illegal invasion. However, I cannot participate in cases where Galactic Congress Signatories are off-ground, and are not detectable by the local authorities. For example, the Krylki Mothership is in geostationary orbit and is cloaked. That is considered legal exploration, and I cannot participate."

"You mean I have to exterminate them by myself?"

"Not exactly. Off the ground, Galactic Representatives are prohibited from employing terminal violence unless the opponents initiate the violence."

"What!" I was incredulous. "They're about to invade Earth and devour the Human population and I'm not allowed to kill them?"

"That is correct, although expressed a bit over-dramatically."

"You bet it's dramatic! Who the hell makes all these dumb rules up, anyway?"

"The rules are imposed by the organization whose name translates into your language as the Congress Responsible for Universal Democracy Everywhere, or CRUD. This organization includes thousands of member species, and it has jurisdiction galaxy-wide. The GPB administers its rules, which pertain to species to species contact and are very complicated."

"Yeah, complicated or not, they don't seem to leave me with any good options," I protested. "Just what am I supposed to do?"

"Skudas Dorval has provided a plan," she said. "And I can provide you with some equipment. Fortunately the Krylki are just initiating their operation so you will find their mothership quite sparsely populated."

When we returned to Pinco F-1, Patricia took me to the recharge room and had me stretch out on the table. "This is where we will provide you with some useful equipment," she said. "First is the Universal Translator Module. This may hurt just a bit." She grasped my earlobe and I felt a sudden sharp pain.

I exclaimed "Ouch, what did you do?" I reached for my ear. There was something there. Patricia showed it to me in a little mirror: she had pierced my ear. I now wore a shiny gold ball in my earlobe. "It translates everything," she explained.

Next she took my right hand, separating out my index finger. She took a thing looking like a huge hypodermic needle and without warning jabbed it into the end of my finger. "Ouch again!"

"It doesn't hurt that much," she admonished. "I have embedded in your finger a laser injector which delivers a serum that inhibits hypnotic effects," Patricia explained: "The Krylki utilize particle effects in their light beams to impose a submissive hypnotic stupor upon their captives. The depth of the stupor permits the aliens to be quite lax in their management of their captives – in effect they are too drugged to do anything beyond what they're told to do."

"And this interferes with that?"

"Yes. The injector I embedded in your finger delivers a drug which moderates or eliminates the hypnotic effect of the light beams. It is most efficient when you inject it by poking your finger lightly against the recipient's cheek." Patricia tapped her cheek by way of demonstration.

She also gave me a can of 'Sweet Evening Breeze' air freshener. "You're kidding," I said. "Is this to cover up the bugs stink or something?"

"No, you must direct the contents of this can into the ventilation system of the mothership. It is a gas which will put the entire crew of the mothership to sleep. It is highly selective and humans will not be affected."

Then she handed me a smartphone, labeled 'Galaxy". "I already have an iPhone," I protested, "With my contacts and all that stuff."

"This device is disguised to appear as a popular brand of a common human device, which the Aliens will recognize as such. In reality it intercepts and manages the navigation system of the Krylki Mothership."

"So I click a button and off they go?" I suspected, not quite so simple.

"It must be activated by your DNA, and additionally requires an accompanying female DNA before it will operate. That is a safety feature that prevents inappropriate use by a single deranged individual, and guarantees usage in a manner approved by the GPB."

Finally we spent some time reviewing the plan for infiltrating the mothership, as provided by Skudas Dorval. We reviewed the blueprints we found on the thumb drive from McGregory's, so I was familiar with the ship's layout. Nevertheless, I was dubious. Very dubious. Since I doubted that the plan was viable, I won't bother with explaining the details. A backup plan came immediately to mind: I hoped to exterminate the aliens, forget the GPB.

As I was taking comfort from the thought of exterminating the aliens, Patricia added, "The Galactic Congress judges a species readiness for open galactic contact largely on the body count of sentient beings when contact first occurs. If you kill them all, Homo Sapiens will be judged too violent for inclusion in Galactic affairs for a very long time."

"So I can't kill them, is that right?" She nodded.

"This is some plan," I proclaimed. Just consider this as indicative of the plan's merits: Although the thumb drive gave lots of information about the mothership's floor plan, it had no information about where the ship was located.   So, in order for me to get onto it, I was going to have to let them kidnap me. You can see how I had my doubts the plan.

Nevertheless, I had no choice. I let them kidnap me.

Chapter 20: Kidnapped

It was clear the aliens were monitoring Greendale, so I went there. I walked slowly into the middle of the backyard and looked up. Not wearing the glasses, of course, I saw nothing.

All at once I was enveloped in a radiant bath of light. Suddenly I felt really lethargic, sort of dazed, like I was half asleep. I don't remember what happened next. I just remember some time later thinking, there's something I need to do. What is it?

Nothing came to mind. Literally, nothing. I was completely thoughtless. But then again I remembered, I need to do something. What? Idly I reached up and scratched my chin. When I did, I noticed a tiny bump on the end of my right index finger. Curious, I looked closer and spotted a little barb like a splinter protruding there.

The finger didn't hurt but it looked sore, so I poked the splinter with my other hand to see if there was pain. "Ouch!" I said aloud...the little sucker bit me sharply. Then very slowly something happened to me, like the cloudy film peeling off your eyes in an allergy pill's advertisement. I began to notice my surroundings. I began to hear sounds, a faint whirring like a well-oiled fan. I sensed an odor – very faint, sort of like skunk cabbage.

To my credit I didn't panic as I became fully aware. I was standing in a brightly lit round room, maybe 30 feet across. The walls, floor and ceiling were completely pale orange. A bench of varied heights circled the room. The floor just in front of me had a large sphincter pattern, like a camera lens. Two cylindrical columns of light ran floor to ceiling, on opposite sides of the room. One column was pale red; the other was pale green.

I was flanked by two little green goblins, like the ones in McGregory's. Across the room another goblin sat at the low spot on the bench. Sitting beside him, on the high part of the bench, was a large blue creature. It was identical to the thing I had melted into water in front of my cousins. Reptilicon, Patricia had called it.

The goblins had very wrinkled green skin and short, knobbed antennae above the big pointy ears. The big black eyes were the only feature on their faces, no nose, no mouth. I guess they weren't just like World of Warcraft goblins after all – those goblins had mouths. Their arms were longer than mine although I was considerably taller than them. They had three spindly fingers on each hand. I couldn't tell anything about sex because they all wore identical gym shorts, black with a white seven-pointed star symbol at the center front.

The blue creature was almost twice the size of the greens. Its skin was made of tiny overlapping pale blue scales that were slightly iridescent. The bulging eyes had vertical black slits in a yellowish orb, like a snake. It blinked sideways. The mouth was huge, like it had a double-hinged jaw. Sure enough, I swear I spotted a forked tongue. It wore a harness with some equipment hanging on it, including a gun-like thing similar to the one fired at me by the fraudulent Deputy Underhill.

As I became gradually more aware of my surroundings, I realized the two aliens sitting across the room were talking. Although the sounds they made were like buzz, whirr, click, pop, click and etc., I understood them fully. I tried my best when translating names, but buzz-click-whirr does not readily come out well in English.

<...Glorious Leader of the Tribe Clara was said to be extremely displeased that the prior expedition returned with the incorrect specimen.> said the goblin. How can it talk without a mouth? I wondered. I made a mental note to ask Patricia.

<No, that specimen was not the galactic representative. A stupid mistake not worthy of the Glorious Leader of the Tribe Clara's little sisters. I thought perhaps one of the little sisters would be punished for their failure, but both were spared.> replied the blue.

<Well, Glorious Leader of the Tribe Clara has already lost three of her seven little sisters to the new galactic representative.> Goblin.

<I suppose she decided she can spare no more.> Blue.

<I pray that we have secured the correct specimen, lest we be subject to discipline.> Goblin.

Just then I felt a little bump, and the whirring noise stopped. The sphincter before me spiraled open and a staired ramp descended ten feet to an orange colored floor below.

<We shall soon know,> said the blue as they both stood up. <We are to deliver him directly to Glorious Leader of the Tribe Clara, and not to the holding pens.>

<I will be honored to bask in her presence,> said the goblin. <If a bit nervous.>

Chapter 21: Prime Sister

The goblins at my sides nudged my elbows, urging me down the stairs. I went. The saucer's ramp closed behind us. I wasn't surprised to confirm that I'd been in a flying saucer. It had landed on three long spindly legs, in a big hanger for flying saucers. I counted eight saucers, including the one I'd been on. Three were stacked one on top of another. Like the saucer's interior, all the surface areas in the hanger were pale orange.

Looking around I noted three double doors on the wall ahead, and the outline of a huge doorway on the wall behind me, big enough for a saucer to exit. High on the wall above the three doors was a long shiny black surface, which I immediately suspected to be one-way glass of some kind.   From the blueprints I'd reviewed with Patricia, I concluded the control room for the hanger was behind the glass.

One goblin led the way, and I followed flanked by the other two, trailed by the blue. We went thru the middle double doorways, into a small room. Across the room two columns of colored light rose into the ceiling, each eight feet across. Their colors were a pale red on the right, and a pale green to the left. The goblin in front stepped into the green light and ascended slowly upward and through the ceiling. As my flankers urged me into the green light, I recognized the purpose of the room and the beams of light: elevators.

We rose through the ceiling into an identical elevator room, but painted a slightly darker orange. Without stopping we continued ascending thru the next ceiling and into yet another elevator room, again slightly darker orange than the one just below. Here my escorts urged me out of the elevating light beam and I stepped forward into the room, with a sensation kind of like getting off an escalator.

We went through a doorway into a tunnel that looked like the passenger entryway onto a 747. It snaked around for thirty or forty feet and led into large enclosure that was open at the top, revealing a roof way overhead. My attention was immediately grabbed by the creature resting on a huge pedestal against the far side of the area.

She was black and shiny, with brilliant streaks of red and orange, and stood over ten feet high. I assumed it was a she, because while I gaped she laid an egg the size of a cantaloupe from the back of her abdomen, plop! It landed near two other eggs on a sort of conveyor belt that appeared to carry the eggs into the next room. A flock of small termite-like bugs the size of big cats shepherded the eggs into neatly spaced order as they moved along with the belt.

I concluded the huge bug was the Prime Sister, since I'd seen her little sisters before, and she looked like them but bigger. Two little sisters identical to the ones I'd seen previously flanked the Prime protectively. The Prime Sister was almost twice their size and loomed over the room like a praying mantis about to pounce. My escorts were visibly frightened, cowering to the side.

Buzz, buzz, click, whirr, click, buzz: the Prime Sister spoke.

<You can understand my words, correct?> she was speaking to me.

"Yes, I can," I managed.

<You are the Homo Sapiens individual who is representative to the Galactic Congress, known as Tom Palmer?> she asked.

While deep in my brain my amygdalae were screaming 'Deny it! Deny it!' I said, "Yes, I am Tom Palmer."

<I am Glorious Leader of the Tribe Clara. I am Prime Sister!>

"Wow! That's a mouthful. Mind if I call you, uh, Clara?" I interrupted.

She reared up, flapping her wings noisily. <You may not! You will address me with respect. Recognize that all on this vessel are my servants. All answer to me! You will be instructed how to address me correctly, if I let you live.>

"Sorry, but we customarily use people's nicknames a lot," I explained.

Her abdomen twitched, vibrated, and swiveled downward to plop another egg onto the conveyer. This didn't interrupt our conversation, as she continued to buzz, click and whirr throughout the egg dropping. <The hierarchy necessary for advanced civilization is thereby lost. This is just my point, Tom Palmer,> she said, <You have apparently leapt to the erroneous conclusion that my people are vicious and cruel savages.>

"And just because you plan to eat my people," I pointed out.

<I shall come back to that,> she said. <You are a pathetically weak species. Any of my sisters could shred you like a head of lettuce,> she commented, and I shivered.

<In spite of your pathetic weakness,> she continued, <you have somehow proceeded to brutally slaughter three of my little sisters. By intergalactic convention, I thereby have the right to subject you to a trial, a prompt guilty conviction, and immediate execution.>.

I noted with surprise that you can sense a threat in a series of buzzes and clicks, because she was definitely threatening me.

I protested. "I claim self-defense. They attacked me. And in addition, you had my father killed."

<Your father's death was a mistake. The clone I sent, Daisy M-752, had orders to subdue him and return him to me. Being generous, I planned to give him a second chance to accept my partnership offer. Daisy M-752 exhibited excessive enthusiasm in the process of subduing. I was annoyed, so I ate Daisy M-752. Thus it is that I must deal with you, Tom Palmer.> She reached across the room with a front limb and touched me gently under the chin.

"My father turned you down, didn't he?"

<He would have reversed his decision! It was made impulsively,> she insisted.

"Your sisters attacked me."

<Nonsense! Their intent was merely to escort you to a meeting with me, peacefully.>

"It sure looked like intent to harm, to me," I protested.

<That lame excuse will not spare you the lethal price of justice. You are clearly guilty. The sentence is death,> She announced. <However, I have decided to be merciful. You see, we Krylki are sophisticated and civilized beings, not primitive savages. Therefore, Tom Palmer, let us pursue negotiation in lieu of conflict. I offer you a deal affording extensive mutual benefits.>

"I can't wait to hear this," I said. "I trust it includes you finding some other planet to exploit."

<No, it does not. The galaxy has very few planets so thoroughly ready to be harvested as this one. Just look at your species! High quality protein in high heels!> I swear she laughed derisively. I found that irritating.

"I understand that harvesting humans would be considered illegal according to galactic standards," I protested.

<It is not illegal if conducted within the terms of a treaty document. So here is your opportunity to

behave as civilized as the Krylki: I offer you a generous partnership. You will remain Galactic representative, and keep the meddling Policy Board out of our business. I will harvest in accordance with a schedule insuring a sustainable supply of nutrients. You may even assume responsibility for selecting the specimens for harvest. It is an opportunity which has proven extremely lucrative in other locations. You would achieve great authority among your kind. Conflict would be minimized.>

She leaned forward, her great triangular head closing in on me, eye facets glistening, mandibles writhing. <Surely you can see the reasonability of such an agreement, Tom Palmer,> she clicked and buzzed right in my face. <Do you need a bit of time to consider friendship?>

I thought about it for a moment. Then the answer came to me: " No, I don't need any time, Clara. Here's my answer: Bug off!" I spat the words into all those glistening facets of her eyeballs.

She reared back angrily. <Stupid uncooperative primitive! You have earned your own extermination, and thereby you have enabled unlimited harvesting of your species to proceed, as fast as we can increase our population.>. Plop: another egg. <Our progress shall be irreversible before the Galactic Congress can

locate and install your successor, who will certainly be more agreeable.> She turned to my escorts. <Take him to the holding pens with the others. Rearrange the processing schedule so that he is used in the next production run.   Good riddance, Tom Palmer!>

They got me out of the room quickly.

Chapter 22: The Holding Pen

The holding pen was down a level. The lead goblin pressed a button and a door slid open, sideways. The other two goblins shoved me through the doorway. The holding pen is a room twenty by thirty, just the one door. The end near the door had a workbench covered with a collection of peoples' possessions, being sorted through by three goblins. I noted that my glasses, squirt gun, can of Sweet Evening Breeze air freshener, and both cell phones were all there. Apparently they had been taken from me when I was in a trance, earlier.

In the middle of the room was a surgical table with large bright lights focused on it. There was a person on the table: Stewart Thorndyke. He appeared to be in a coma.

Standing across the room were five more people, including Sophia. I was greatly relieved to see that she appeared unharmed, although in a deep trance, staring off into infinity. I took her hand and said hello, but she didn't seem to notice. Gently I poked her cheek with the barb on my index finger, and watched as her eyes gradually refocused from infinity down to me.

"Tom!" she exclaimed. I could see she was surprised and confused.

"Sophia. Are you okay?" I asked.

"I think so. Where are we? The last thing I remember was driving up to your father's house." Then she noticed the goblins at the workbench, across the room. Her eyes got big. "Omigod!"

As we watched, one of the goblins took an object from the table, examined it briefly, then deposited it into a slot atop a squat black garbage can beside the table. There was a flash of light and a sizzling sound and the object was gone.

"We've been kidnapped by aliens." I informed her. "But relax. We're going to escape."

I tried a reassuring smile but I wasn't sure it worked, for either her or me.

She whispered. "You were right. You did see aliens at McGregory's. Why didn't I?"

"The aliens disguise themselves to look just like people by wearing a doohickey which distorts peoples' eyesight. My glasses eliminate the distortion, but they only work with my DNA."

"And I didn't believe you. I'm sorry," she said.

I nodded. "I understand. What were you doing at Greendale? That's where they caught you."

She reached in a pocket and drew out a piece of paper. "After we argued, I found this. It's a note from your father. I had it from your jacket pocket, from when I tranquilized you last night. I'd forgotten it." She handed me the paper.

Suddenly I recalled the note I'd picked up when I'd first met Patricia. I took the paper from Sophia and read:

Tom, be warned. Blue aliens are assassins. Green aliens select kidnap victims. All of them will be out to get you. I have discovered that whistling a song is often helpful.

Your father,

Jack Forsome'.

Sophia said, "When I read that, I decided I'd been too hard on you and I wanted to apologize. I was sure you'd be at Greendale, so I went there. Then the car stalled on the way down the driveway, and I don't remember anything else until just now. Tom, what are we going to do?"

I showed her the barb on my index finger. "This relieves the hypnotic effect generated by the lights the aliens use on us. I'm going to apply it to the other people here. Then we're all going to get out of here."

I recalled that the aliens expected us to be pretty much stationary and docile as an effect of the light beam hypnosis, so I was concerned that the goblins would react to my moving around too much, and I tried to move very slowly. Two of the other people I recognized; they were the older couple who had come into McGregory's just after Sophia and me. They looked like they could be someone's grandparents. The other two people looked like a brother and sister, with matching dark hair. All four people were large.

I cautioned everybody to remain calm until I got them out of there. I was hoping I could do that. Everybody seemed to be okay, except the dark-haired brother who said, "I remember just eating, but now I'm starving." His sister said, "Oh, you're always hungry, Tim."

"Whatever you do, don't eat the chocolate mint cookies," I advised. "They won't sit well."

The last person I awakened was Thorndyke, flat on his back on the table. By now the goblins were watching me, but they didn't seem overly alarmed. I guessed that they just didn't expect any trouble from their tranquilized animals.

I recalled he'd been stung rather than tranquilized by light beam, but I hoped that the serum injected by my finger would revive him anyway. I held him down when I poked his cheek, so he wouldn't jump right off the table as he came out of the trance. I was relieved to see the injection was working. As his eyes slowly cleared, I whispered, "Take it easy. We don't want to alarm the guards."

He relaxed and glanced around, taking in the goblins and people. "We're in a saucer," he observed quietly. I let him sit up slowly.

"Not quite. It's their mothership," I corrected.

He shook his head in disgust. "I'm not getting paid enough for this," He said.

"Me neither," I agreed.

He nodded toward the three goblins at the workbench. "We can take them."

"No, we're not permitted to kill them. We need to disable them, so we can gather our stuff and get out of here."

"What? Why can't we just kill them?" he insisted.

"Uh, because it's considered really bad form under the rules of the Galactic Congress."

He'd been staring at the goblins. Now he turned his stare on me. He looked at for what seemed a really long time. Finally he shrugged. "If you say so," he conceded. "That sounds like something your father would say. But then, how are we going to disable them?"

"The note from my father suggested whistling. That sounds thoroughly preposterous to me, but what the hell. Let's try that first." I pursed my lips and blew. No noise. My lips were dry as the Sahara. I wet them with my tongue and tried again. Nothing. Whistling sure wasn't going to work if I couldn't make any noise. Thorndyke tried too, and failed more completely than me.

Sophia had been talking to the others, but now she came over to us. "What on earth are you two trying to do?"

"Whistle."

"Whistle?"

I nodded. "Whistle. Like this." I blew. Nothing came out. I was getting frustrated.

"You mean like this?" Sophia whistled. She whistled strong and loud and wonderfully in tune. She whistled 'Yankee Doodle Dandy', three verses of it, and then moved on to 'Oh What a Beautiful Morning.'

I checked out the Goblins. Amazingly, they were totally enraptured by Sophia's whistling, like they'd never before heard anything so wonderful. They moved closer and stared while she serenaded them. Their big ears wiggled in time to the music. I couldn't believe it. Their bulging eyes bulged even bigger as they watched her whistle. Their mouths would have been gaping, if only they had mouths.

Sophia finished 'a Beautiful Morning' and started in on South Pacific: 'Some Enchanted Evening' was first. The Goblins were so thoroughly engrossed that I had no problem sidling around them and moving to the workbench. Quickly I picked up my glasses, squirt gun, air freshener, and both cell phones: my original iPhone and the fake Galaxy from Patricia.

I turned the squirt gun's dial to yellow, to disable the Goblins instead of killing them. They had their backs to me, watching raptly while Sophia whistled 'I'm Gonna Wash That Man Right Outa My Hair". It occurred to me, that I could easily 'Wash these goblins right outta my hair,' permanently. All I had to do was turn the gun's dial to green. Only reluctantly did I decide to save that strategy in case we had to move to a plan B.

Zap, zap, zap. Pale yellow tinged donuts burst from the squirt gun and encased each of the goblins. Inside the shiny yellow encasement, the goblins gently collapsed to the floor, like in slow motion. Once down, they looked like they were sleeping, each sprawled in a limp bundle.

Everybody gathered their belongings from the workbench, quickly, stepping carefully around the goblins on the floor. Grandma and Grandpa had his and her handbags. Thorndyke had the most stuff, including handcuffs, bully club, taser gun, flashlight and a cell phone.

The door out of the holding pen was locked, of course. There was a panel goblin-high along the right side of the door, featuring two odd looking spots, one red and one yellow.

"Hit the button, let's get outta here," Thorndyke urged, pointing at the spots on the panel.

"Which button?" I asked.

Thorndyke didn't hesitate. "This one." He said impatiently. He stepped up and pressed the red button firmly. Nothing happened, so he at once hit the yellow button. Again nothing happened. "Damn!" he swore.

"I believe one button opens the door; the other is an alarm. And evidently the aliens have wired the cage door so that we animals can't open the door," I commented. "Good thing, isn't it, otherwise you'd have set off the alarm, Thorndyke."

"Well then, you get the door open, genius." He was unapologetic.

"Note that the buttons are not shaped like a human finger," I observed. The buttons were a narrow oblong shape, too narrow for human digits. The goblins, I realized, had long slender fingers. So I stepped over to the closest goblin and took it by the arm. I nodded to the dark-haired brother, Tim, standing there, "Take its other arm and help me drag it to the door," I said.

By the door, I looked closer at the buttons. The red looked to have been used a lot more often than the yellow, so I pressed the goblin's finger against the red button. I was relieved to see the door slide silently leftward and into the wall.

Chapter 23: Control Room

I remembered the path we had followed when I was brought to the holding pen, earlier. Reversing that, we needed to turn left out of the door of the holding pen, then take the first right and proceed down that hall. A door at the far end should lead to the room with the elevators at the center of the mothership.

"I think I know the way," I said, "Follow me." I stepped through the doorway, turning left along the hall. There were four other doors into holding pens, all open and empty. I was thankful the aliens didn't have a bunch more people stashed away.

We turned the corner, heading toward the elevator room. This hall was twenty feet long, and had a door at the far end, with a small window. The door at the end had the same yellow and red button arrangement as the holding pen door. Looking at the fingerprint panel, I realized we would need to drag a sleeping goblin around with us, applying its finger to the buttons that opened the doors, in order to get around the ship.

While Thorndyke and Tim went back for a goblin, I peered carefully through the window. The pale red and green vertical columns of light confirmed that I was looking into the elevator room for this level.

Fortunately it was empty. As Patricia had forecast, the ship seemed to be sparsely populated.

There was a door directly across the elevator room that looked like the one I was looking through. From the blueprints I expected that door would lead to the mothership's main equipment compartments – engines, ventilation, plumbing, and so on. We would need to access the ventilation system in there, to use the 'air freshener'.

Thorndyke and Tim arrived with the limp goblin and I applied its finger to the red button. The door slid open. Quickly we crossed to the other door. The same trick with the goblin's finger had it open promptly, and we all filed into a hallway perpendicular to the axis of the mother ship. Three large doors were spaced along the wall across the hall. They looked to be double swinging doors.

From my review of the blueprints I decided the door to the right led into the chamber housing the ventilation equipment. I was nervous about the crowd of seven people traipsing around an alien mothership, so I was impatient and barged right through the door and into a big room cluttered with varied machinery and ductwork.

Off to the right three goblins had the panel removed from the front of a furnace-like machine. I'm not sure who was more startled, me or them, but I had the advantage with my squirt gun already in hand. Zap! One disabled. Zap! Second disabled.

But when I squeezed the trigger aiming at the third goblin, nothing happened. I looked at the gun. I shook it. It was empty! Meanwhile the third goblin came at me, snarling, grabbing with its long spindly arms. How could it snarl with no mouth, I wondered again. But it definitely was snarling.

<Buzz, Whirr, click, click,> it cried out, <Stand aside! G-662 must alert security! Security will subdue the intruders,> It buzzed noisily. I realized it wasn't fighting me so much as trying to reach the yellow button on the panel by the door. I struggled to keep it away, but despite my height advantage the thing was considerably stronger than me; I was losing. It stabbed its finger against the wall behind me, just missing the yellow button.

Then suddenly it began vibrating madly. I let it go and it collapsed to the floor, convulsing. It was flopping like a tuna on the deck of a fishing boat. I realized Thorndyke was standing next to me, taser in hand. "Looks like tasers work pretty good on these buggers," he said. "Why do they always come in groups of three?"

"Because that way, one of each of their three sexes is represented in every group." I proposed.

Thorndyke was astonished. "I didn't know they had any sexes, let alone three! What's the third sex?"

"I haven't got a clue. I was just joking." I admitted. "Anyway, let's get on with our business."

Promptly we located the bank of intake manifolds which bypassed the airflow filters. I removed the cap from the can of 'Sweet Evening Breeze' air freshener. The can had threads which matched those on the intake manifold. As I screwed the can onto the manifold, the can's trigger was depressed and we all heard a phhhht as the can gradually emptied into the mothership's air system.

Shortly we all noticed a slight aroma which hadn't been there previously, replacing the skunk cabbage smell. It did smell like a sweet evening breeze, for sure. Theoretically it meant that all aliens aboard were knocked out, and that our escape was assured. Things seemed to be looking up.

I led the gang back to the elevator room and explained that the green beam of light went up; the red went down. "I need to go to the control room, which is at the top of the ship," I told them.

"Does everybody need to go to the control room?" asked grandpa.

"Maybe somebody should be looking for a way out of here," Thorndyke suggested.

"But Tom is the only one who knows his way around the ship," Sophia pointed out. "And I think we should stay together."

"Whichever, we should hurry," Thorndyke exclaimed. "This place is making me really nervous!"

"Oh, you're just being a tepee and a wigwam at the same time," I told him.

"What's that supposed to mean?"

"You're just too tense," I deadpanned. The crowd groaned in unison. Thorndyke just shook his head.

Finally we all agreed together was safer, although it was clear that most of them were getting very anxious to be out of there. Not that I could blame them. So we stepped into the green beam of light and gently ascended.

The next level up was the level where I'd met the Prime Sister, earlier. The level was 30 feet or more floor to ceiling, and once we had ascended above the entryway into the gangway leading to the Prime Sister, we had a clear view of the entire level until we passed up through the floor to the level above.

We were uniformly appalled, even though all the creatures seemed to be asleep, as we hoped. About the size of a football field, the entire level was populated with bugs of varied size and shape, evidently representing the entire life cycle of the Krylki: egg, larva, pupa, hatchling and adult. The place was crawling with them, although they weren't crawling right now because they were sleeping. The Prime Sister rested in her chamber, attended by the sleeping little bugs that looked like termites, and two little sisters. The conveyer onto which she laid eggs circled the entire room.

There were racks where eggs had been placed, awaiting hatching. The few hatched larva further along the belt were fat brown blobs, perhaps a yard long, shaped like grubs. Next to that were more termite-like bugs, the pupa, which had evidently been busy wrapping themselves into cocoons when they fell asleep. Filled cocoons were hung in rows along the walls. Finally we saw a handful of Krylki hatchlings, freshly out of cocoons. These cuties were half the size of the adult 'little' sisters; I guess they took a lot of chocolate mint cookies to get big.

I was afraid for a moment that some of us might get sick at the sights in the Krylki reproduction deck. Fortunately, we ascended fast enough that we didn't have to observe the horrors any longer than a minute or so.

The elevators rose through the floor into the level above. It was an empty room similar to the one two decks down. Slightly darker orange color, as expected.

Then we ascended into the control room, where the elevator light beam stopped lifting us, gently ejecting just at floor level. Curiously, the room was dark, except for a few display lights here and there on equipment at the perimeter of the room. I suddenly felt nervous. Then the red and green light beams of the elevators blinked off, leaving what appeared to be solid floor.

The lights in the room brightened. It was a round room, maybe thirty feet across. I saw with dismay that we were surrounded. Two Sisters, three blue lizard men, and three green goblins were spread in a circle around us. I noted that many of the aliens had drawn weapons.

<Buzz, click, hiss, tick, tock,> one of the 'little" sisters stepped forward and spoke. <You are caught. I have disabled the elevators so you cannot escape. We have observed your progress through our home with great amusement. But now your adventure is over.>

"What happened to the sleeping gas?" hissed Thorndyke.

He was talking to me, but the Sister answered. "<I arranged for this deck to have additional filters for its air supply. Therefore your poison did not affect this level. I have earned great prestige with this victory! Remember my name: Yummy Bambi!>

At first I thought it was a sneeze, but then I realized she was boasting. She followed this with what I took to be a bugs' form of laughter: <click, ping, beep, toot, tick, tock>.

I chimed in with "Gesundheit!" anyway.

She paid no attention, and continued. <You are all doomed. Your weapon is empty. You are no match for us physically. I shall sting you into submission at my pleasure. In 32.5 of your minutes the effect of your poison in our air will end. Our companions will

waken. Then we will remove you to the holding pens for immediate processing. The resulting nutrients will be very timely for rapidly expanding our population.>

"What did it say?" asked Sophia.

Thorndyke answered first. "It plans to kill us and then eat us."

"Can you understand them?" I was surprised.

"No, but it seems a pretty good guess," Thorndyke answered. "Am I right?"

"Pretty much," I nodded.

Things looked bad. They were mostly bigger and quicker than us, and even the little green goblins were stronger than me. I didn't see how we could defeat them. Thorndyke's taser could not handle all eight before they got him. Even if we did overcome them, in half an hour when the other aliens awakened, we had to be off the ship. I was coming up empty as far as our next move.

Finally I thought I might try negotiating, but before I could get started, Grandma stepped out in front of me, her hand stuck deep in her handbag.

"Think again, buggy!" she exclaimed, surprising everyone in the room. "Come on Pappy, let's gettem!" She whipped a little pink canister out of her handbag, held it up at arm's length, and expertly sprayed a 10 foot long thick stream of dark colored liquid directly into the face of the Sister taunting us. Almost instantly I knew what it was: the heavy smell of pepper filled the room. Grandma expertly and rapidly sprayed a wide arc of pepper juice, catching all of the aliens facing her in turn, before any of them could react. Grandpa did the same on the other side of the room.

It was over in seconds. The primary effects of pepper spray are painfully swollen eyes with blindness, difficulty breathing, and panic. The effect must have been really terrible on the collection of huge bulging alien eyeballs. The aliens forgot us completely. They were all desperately thrashing about, totally helpless while trying to avoid the disabling effect on the pepper spray, to no avail.

"Thank goodness for Pop Club," Grandpa commented, carefully wiping the residual pepper spray from the nozzle of his blue pepper spray canister with a tissue.

"What's the Pop Club?" Sophia asked.

"The Paranoid Old People's Club. They hold self-defense classes for seniors. That's where Gammy and I learned how to use the pepper spray so well."

"You clearly learned well," I commented.

All we had to do was get the thrashing aliens under control, somehow. Then I noticed a liquid dispenser, like a water dispenser in an office where people discuss the latest episode of 'The Walking Dead', on the wall nearby. If it was water I could reload. I tasted a couple drips with my finger...Thank god, it was water. Rapidly I reloaded the squirt gun and used the yellow setting to restrain the collection of aliens. At last they all lay immobilized and sleeping around the control room floor.

Next I used the Galaxy cell phone supplied by Patricia to interface with the ships' main navigation system. I pressed the 'on' button and the phone's display advised that I was about to download and install a navigational program that would direct the mothership to accelerate out of our solar system. Patricia had estimated that it would take the Krylki at least three days to interrupt the navigation program. Since their main engines provided speeds at a multiple of light speed, they would by then be far away from Earth. Moving with enormous momentum, it would be impossible to reverse course.

We merely had to follow the instructions on the Galaxy's screen. I could set the time before the program initiated ignition of the ship's engines; I chose 25 minutes. Just before all the aliens woke up.

The pseudo cell phone posed the question: 'Are you sure you want to perform this action? Y/N.'

I selected Y.

The cell phone flashed a new message. It said, "In order to verify compliance with CRUD regulations, proper verification of your authority is required. Proceed Y/N?

I typed Y.

Next Message; 'The individual providing authorization #1: place your thumb on the circle displayed below. (Note: This individual must be the Galactic Representative.) A circle the size of a half dollar appeared at the phone's lower right corner.

I right thumbed where indicated.

'The individual providing authorization #2: place your thumb on the circle displayed below. (Note: This individual must be same species as #1, but of opposite sex.) A circle appeared at the phone's lower left corner.

I nodded to Sophia and she stepped forward and looked at the circle. "What's it doing?" she whispered.

"It's going to shoot this ship and all the aliens into outer space. I believe it just takes two to tango," I suggested.

"You mean, to set it off? This is going to be strange, isn't it?" she asked.

"I'm pretty sure, given stuff that's happened the last couple of days, that it is going to be totally strange. But if you hold my hand, I know that we'll get through OK." I held out my left hand.

Sophia smiled at me and took my hand firmly in her right hand. "Okay, let's tango!" she said with a grin. She plopped her left thumb on the indicated circle.

Immediately everything went black. Sophia's face surrounded by total darkness was the only thing I could see. Shocked, I clutched her hand; she clutched back. Together we clutched the Galaxy pseudo phone. Then a milky way of stars appeared, far away, swirling rapidly in a huge circle around us. They increased speed and blurred into a belt of light rapidly spinning around us, enclosing us in a glowing cloud.

After a few seconds I sensed the presence of others around us, lots of others, joining and participating in the experience with us. Somehow I knew these others were people, but not just Homo sapiens, they were all kinds of strange and exotic sentient peoples. As the light spun around us, I seemed to become intermingled with them all, and with Sophia. I sensed then that we were being assessed, and that vast multitudes were sharing our thoughts and experience.

While all of this was happening, somehow, miraculously, I touched Sophia's soul, and she touched mine. I know this sounds inexcusably and unbelievably mystical, but we both knew what we felt. We were forever changed by sharing this experience.

As I marveled at what was happening to us, I sensed a growing approval all around us, and then an agreement was reached. With that, the beings faded out of our consciousness, the stars around us slowed their swirling and gradually disappeared, and the darkness faded away.

I could only stare at Sophia, hand in hand. The experience had let us touch each other in a way beyond what most people can ever know. I could see it in the astonished, happy expression lighting her face.

I heard a voice, as if in the distance, "Hello? Hello? Are you two alright?" It was Thorndyke.

"I don't think we could be any better than this," I told him. I laughed, and Sophia laughed with me.

"Well listen, if you can stop mooning at each other, we probably should get out of here, don't you think?" Thorndyke urged.

I glanced at Patricia's cell phone. A message was on the screen:

Authorizing Individuals Successfully Validated.

CRUD Approval Achieved.

Download Completed.

Ignition will commence in:

20:28 Minutes

"You're right; we need to be moving right along." I agreed. "Let's go."

Chapter 24 Escape

We found the elevator controls and turned the down elevator to the 'on' setting. We filed into the pale red light beam and gently descended through all levels to the bottom, where the flying saucer hanger was located. We burst out of the elevator room and into the hanger. Five saucers sat idle but with lights blinking, waiting to carry us to safety. The three in a stack were unlighted, and didn't look ready to fly. We noted a crew of three goblins sleeping on the floor near the stacked saucers.

First problem: we had no idea how to get into a flying saucer, let alone fly it. Looking around for inspiration, I saw the window for the hanger's control room and decided to investigate there. Stairs in the elevator room led up to the control room and we found out that it was more like a ready room.

Three blue lizard-men were stretched out sleeping on the floor, fallen where our gas had caught them. From somewhere I remembered that the blues were pilots. Then I noticed each of the sleeping blues wore a chain necklace with a doohickey like an automobile fob hung at the end. Urged on by Thorndyke, I hastily collected all three fobs from the blue pilots, and headed back to the hanger.

Examining the fobs, I noted each had the outline of a seven pointed star on one side – the Krylki symbol. More cryptic symbols were etched inside the seven pointed stars. These symbols differed on each pilot's fob. Opposite the starred side of the fob was an indentation that by now I readily recognized as an alien fingerprint groove.

I gathered the group and showed them the fobs. "We need to figure how these work," I said. "See these symbols?" I pointed to the seven pointed star. "These match symbols on the saucers. Then the pilot's fingerprint in this groove activates the respective saucer."

"I get it," said Tim. "We need to match the correct finger to the matching fob and saucer."

"Doesn't that mean we have to lug the bodies from upstairs down to the saucers?" Sophia said with dismay.

"Not really." Thorndyke said. "I have a sharp knife. We just need the fingers." He held up a knife that looked plenty sharp and big enough to hack off a finger.

"No way! I do not want to know the color of their blood! Disgusting!" Sophia protested.

"But those lizards are heavy," Thorndyke.

A chorus of nos. "Majority rules. We'll carry them as needed." I summed it up.

We hurriedly lugged the pilots down from the control room and started checking saucers. The big blues were a lot heavier than the greens. I glanced at Patricia's cell phone: 12:15.

We had to run around the hanger matching the pilots and the fobs to the appropriate saucers. Once a fob and a saucer were paired, we tried fingers from each pilot in turn. At the first fob/saucer match, none of the pilots' fingers made anything happen. Same at the second. And at the third.

Something was missing. We were getting desperate. 10:20 on the phone. Brother Tim had the answer. "It's a double coded authentication system, to improve security. Like having a password and an access code. I believe that somewhere there's an on/off switch that must be on for the fobs to operate." He told us.

The control room seemed the logical place to find the master switch, and we rushed back up the stairs. Right away we recognized where the switch was located: in a locked metal console.

"We've got to find a key" I cried.

"No time for that," Thorndyke countered.   He stepped up to the console and bashed the lock with his bully club. The lock crashed to the floor and the console flew open, revealing a row of twelve red levers, all in the down position.

Which one? Never mind, I rapidly flipped all twelve levers to the up position. In the hanger below a succession of humming sounds began. The saucers were all warming up.

6:30

"Let's get back to the pilots and their fobs," I said.

We dashed back down the stairs to the hanger and a collected a set of one pilot, one saucer, and one matching fob. Shove a pilot's finger on the fob: nothing. Switch to the next pilot: Success!

The saucer's sphincter swirled open. The staired ramp dropped down from the belly and we scrambled aboard. I jumped into the green light beam elevator and ascended into the cockpit. Room for three. Sophia and Thorndyke followed me up and the others settled on the deck below.

Like the TeeDee at Dr. Forsome's home, the dashboard had joysticks left and right, and a green button in the center. Patricia had said the technology was similar. I stabbed the green button without hesitation. Nothing happened.

"Dammit!" I realized the problem. "We need the pilot's finger!" Down the elevator, down the ramp, lug the pilot back up to the cockpit.

4:15

In our haste we dropped the poor alien three times before we got its long blue finger on the green button.

A somewhat harsh, sort of feminine voice said <chirp, cluck, peep, giggle, click.>. Translated: <Instructions?>

"Take us to the home of Dr. Jack Forsome," Optimistic, but I thought I'd give it a shot.

<Secondary validation is required to authorize an alternate flight director.>

3:07

"What does that mean?" Thorndyke sounded desperate.

"Let's just get the pilot's finger on the button again and hope it works," I said.

It did work. <Validation accepted. I am Iwupsa Ahgechku, automated manager of this vehicle. Shall I proceed as per previous instruction?>

1:45

"Yes!" I heard the ramp closing below.

"Wait! How are we going to get out of the hanger? We need to open the hanger door or something. We can' just crash through the wall!" Thorndyke said.

"Oh no? Just watch - I have a good feeling about this," I reassured him. It was going to work like the TeeDee, right?

The saucer started moving slowly across the hanger floor.

:35

"Hurry UP!" I insisted.

The saucer abruptly accelerated rapidly, rushing directly at the hanger wall. But instead of an impact, the saucer passed harmlessly through the solid wall and out into space. We made a grand circle as Whoopsy or whatever-her-name was laid out a course down into the Earth's atmosphere toward Greendale.

Thus we were looking at the mothership, a big motionless blob, when Patricia's Galaxy phone announced: 'Ignition is commencing...now.'

The mothership began to glow as its engines built power. It began to move, at first slowly. Then it pulled a thing like the starship Enterprise when Sulu hits the Warp button. Whoosh, off it went, a streak of light quickly vanishing into the distance.

From there it was no problem riding the saucer on a course back....home. I found that my cell phone worked, and I made a couple of calls along the way.

After about thirty minutes, at last we spotted the house. We spiraled down to a soft landing in the middle of the backyard. Once the saucer settled, we clambered down the ramp, heading toward the house. I saw my calls had worked: a crowd of people surged around the house and closed in: Attorney Smith and his receptionist, Marty Wilson, Robbie Johnson, Sophia's son. Aunt Sally and my two cousins, Troy and Larry.

As the groups came together, I turned back to the saucer sitting in my backyard. I pulled out my squirt gun, turned the dial to red, pointed it at the saucer and pulled the trigger. A whirling vortex surged from the muzzle and rapidly expanded, flashing with bright white light tinged with red spots. By the time it reached the saucer it was large enough to completely engulf it, and for a moment the whole thing shimmered and sizzled there on the grass. Then with a huge gurgling sound it all collapsed into a deluge of water, soaking the entire backyard.

The crowd of people gasped in surprise. In a chorus several demanded, "Why did you do that?"

I told them, "Because, there are no such things as Aliens."

Locust Area Shopping News: Several citizens claim to have witnessed a flying saucer crash early this morning, near the Forsome Estate. Authorities have officially denied these reports, stating that no conclusive evidence has been found. Furthermore, area Meteorologists report that unusual cloud formations were observed in that area, and are likely the cause of the sightings.

Chapter 20: Happily ever;

Afterward, there was a short meeting in Greendale's dining room. At my call earlier, Attorney Smith had gathered Aunt Sally and together they retrieved my father's amended Will from the safe deposit box. It turned out that Aunt Sally and Marty Wilson had signed the will as witnesses to my father's signature, so the validity of the will was pretty much beyond question.

Attorney Smith had also picked up my DNA results from IdentityDNA.com, confirming that my earlier test was correct. I didn't really need it since my father's will specifically stated that anyone whose finger could open his vault at Greendale was to be considered his direct descendent. I had plenty of witnesses to that. The will appointed me and Attorney Smith as co-executers.

My cousins Troy and Larry were getting pretty sullen, until we got to the part where my father created trust accounts for each, conditional upon them agreeing to not contest his latest will. Once they heard the dollar amounts involved, they readily agreed. It was going to take them quite some time to spend it all.

The foundation for assisting selected children also received permanent funding. Marty Wilson was visibly relieved.

You might think there wouldn't be much left over for me, but that's not so. I received the rights to a handful of patents which generated a substantial income, and ownership of Greendale, my father's residence, including all contents, especially the vault.

My cousin's idea of turning it into a pub was dead. I was pretty sure I was going to move in. And if I did ever decide to sell, I knew for sure who was going to get the contract: she wasn't letting go of my hand. And I wasn't letting go of her hand, either.

There was a fleeting moment when I thought, 'there goes my quiet life as a bachelor', but then I realized I was looking forward to a changed life involving adventure, sharing, and discovery. All I needed was to have a good bit of fun along the way.